FANCY ANDERS GOES TO WAR

WHO KILLED ROSIE THE RIVETER?

MAX ALLAN COLLINS

Art by
FAY DALTON

Cover design by
WBYK

NeoText

Published by NeoText, 2021
Text copyright © 2021 Max Allan Collins
Art copyright © 2021 Fay Dalton

All rights reserved. No part of this publication may be reproduced or transmitted in any form or by any means without permission of the author.

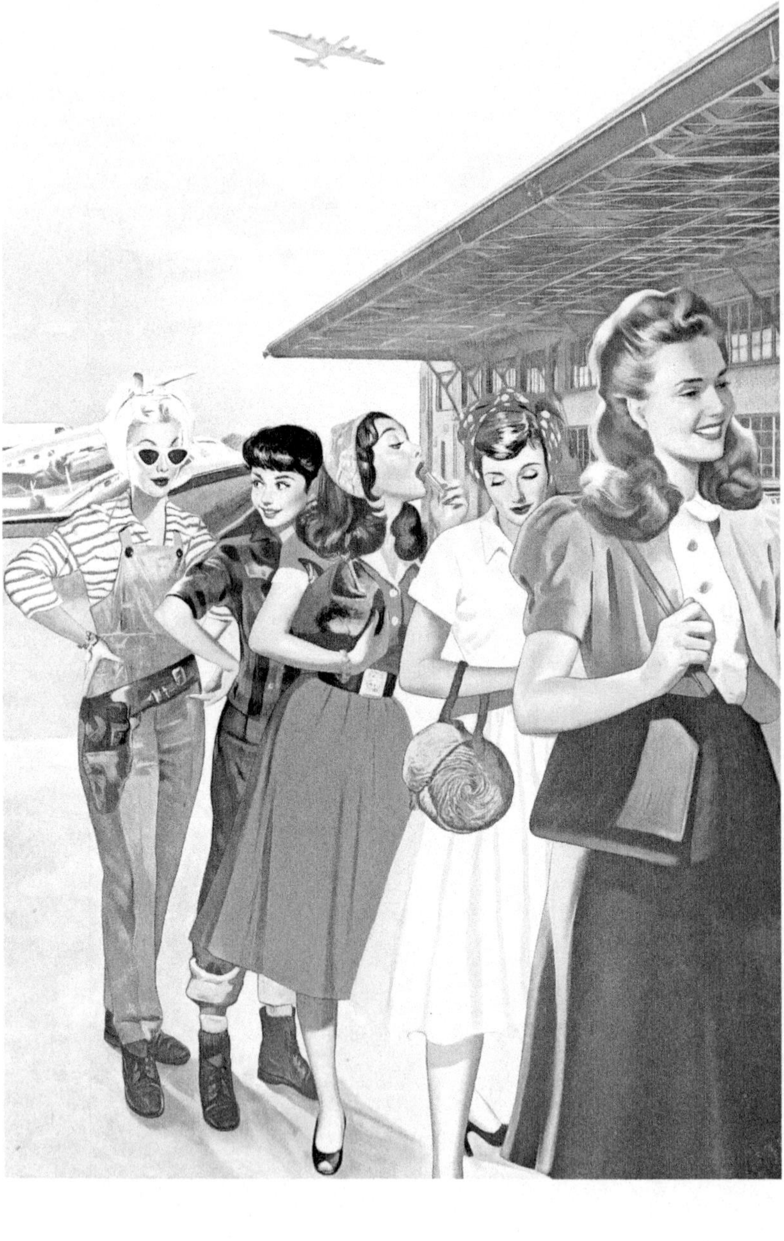

1

SWING SHIFT

Fancy Anders, in an endless line of women outside the Amalgamated Aircraft plant, had all the required proof of identity a first-time war worker needed (birth certificate, driver's license, and Social Security card), none of it bearing her real name.

As far as anyone asking was concerned, she was Franny Allison, just another young woman showing up for the first day of a defense job either out of patriotism or the lure of sixty-eight cents an hour...or both.

Not that Fancy needed sixty-eight cents. At twenty-four, she was a very well-fixed young lady, and – although she hadn't intended it – that fact showed, and how. Wearing baby-blue coveralls with a red-striped white top, she had parked her pink Packard convertible in the six-thousand-car capacity lot, sporting a much-envied C-ration sticker – *Essential hospital, utility, or war worker*, a designation few at this plant were lucky enough to hold.

All around her were girls and women, jitterbugs and housewives, in short sleeves and slacks, summery dresses and open-toed heels, though this was a morning in early fall, 1942. Of course summer was a state of mind in Southern California, where any female – whether in bobby sox or white gloves – was welcome to try her hand at war work.

Fancy, who stood out in this crowd, was very blonde, if rather more so than nature had in mind, slender, curvy, with long legs that did not stop her from wearing heels. Her features were seemingly on loan from the late Carole Lombard, with the exception of a spare pair of Betty Grable's red-rouged lips. Her nearly platinum tresses were pinned up in a pile, hidden by a white turban; her almond-shaped light-blue eyes with their long, natural lashes, were similarly hidden away by big white-framed sunglasses.

None of this bought her anything but a place at the end of the line. She fell in behind a girl whose trim five-foot-four figure was arranged in a red-and-black plaid blouse, cuffed denims, and hard-toed work boots. This confident creature turned to Fancy, revealing herself as a pug-nosed cutie with big dark eyes and a bigger bright smile.

"Staying overnight?" the cutie asked.

Fancy was lugging a big canvas duffel that was as utilitarian as everything else about her wasn't.

"Nope," Fancy said. "Just a handbag got out of hand."

"Sure, why not? Some bum makes a pass, you can hit him with your purse, and *mean* it."

Fancy, liking her already, extended a hand. "Franny Allison. Pasadena."

They shook.

"Lula Hall, Hollywood."

"Actress?"

"About the only thing I haven't tried. Roller-skating carhop, bowling alley pin setter...gas pump jockey, of late. You?"

"My daddy's secretary," she said, which was sort of true. True enough.

"Sugar Daddy?"

"No. Actual daddy."

Lula made an appreciative face. "Nice work if you can get it. Why trade that in for a rivet gun?"

"Daddy's shut his office down for the duration. Got called back to active duty." Also not wholly untrue. Exactly what kind of office didn't come up yet, nor what duty. "Thought I should do my bit."

Lula thrust a forefinger at her. "'Uncle Sam Needs You.' You can work your way up in this joint to a buck five, I hear."

"No kidding." Fancy's salary from her father was five hundred a month.

The line was moving fairly fast. Helmeted soldiers with rifles walked guard duty up and down and back again. The many formidable buildings beyond the chain-link fence were painted a dull flat green, sandbags piled all around. Fancy and Lula were moving under a canopy of camouflage netting, more of which draped the looming buildings. On top of a low-slung structure, down by where they'd be checked through, an anti-aircraft nest was stationed, two GIs at a big gun, another fanning the sky with binoculars.

"You know what I heard?" Lula asked, walking backward. She was chewing gum and snapped it from time to time.

"No. What?"

"You fly over this place in a plane? Looks like Carville – you know, Andy Hardy's hometown?"

"How so?"

"Well, I heard girls talking at the Studio Hotel, which is where I live, and they say Paramount sent set designers down to make canvas-and-plywood houses and chicken-wire trees and paint streets to put on top of these buildings. To make the Nips think, when they invade? That this is just some quiet boring neighborhood."

"Must be that movie magic you hear so much about."

At the gate, the line swarmed, and one by one the young women had their temporary ID cards and belongings (purses, lunch boxes, Fancy's duffel) checked by armed police-style guards, who then herded them up to a ten-foot cement wall garnished with electrified barbed wire. As they stood milling, Fancy and Lula chatted, both hiding their apprehension.

"Where did you train?" Lula asked. "I took classes at Hollywood High, nights, for a month. Welding and riveting."

"Vocational School in Downey. Amalgamated has a plant near there." She did not mention that her training had been for one intense single week by a select tutor.

Lula asked, "But you picked Long Beach instead?"

"Better opportunities, I heard." True enough, but not why Fancy was here.

An efficient woman in her fifties, who had already managed early in the day to achieve an impressive level of boredom, passed out manila envelopes plump with handbooks, pamphlets, lists of work clothes, regulations and tools to acquire, plus the latest *Amalgamated Employee News* and an aircraft union membership card.

"Any questions you may have," the woman said, "are answered in that envelope. In the meantime, line up and follow that yellow line."

That took them down a hallway to an infinite office where dozens and dozens of desks and harried-looking women, often with glasses, always with typewriters, awaited. There Fancy's false name and Lula's real one were recorded.

The two young women (and the others) were sent from this desk to that one, for job and pay rate classification, physical description documentation, birth certificate check, time clock instruction, identification card signing, then visits to little rooms for fingerprinting, ID badge photography, and a cursory physical exam.

Last stop was another, smaller office where each applicant was made to read, and sign, the Espionage Act, Executive Act of the President of the United States – *Secret, Confidential and Restricted*. Fancy, under false pretenses here, allowed herself to feel a little intimidated by that one.

Then the new workers were presented with big yellow political campaign-style buttons, with the numbers of their assigned departments. Both Fancy and Lula, perhaps because they'd gone through all of this together, received the same number: 190.

A man in his forties in a tan jumpsuit played weary Pied Piper to the women, leading them up a flight of stairs into an auditorium with college-style tiered seating. Fancy and Lula sat up close.

At a lectern in front of a pulled-down movie screen, the man in tan rattled off facts (the facility had cost twelve million and its fifteen concrete-and-steel buildings, connected by tunnels, weighed 9000 tons) and showed a few slides, primarily of the aircraft built in Long Beach (DB-7 attack plane, B-24 long-range bomber, C-47 cargo hauler).

"Now we'll have a double feature," he said, with the enthusiasm of a principal at an assembly making a little joke that even he didn't think was funny.

The first of two classroom-style films showed an airplane being built by thousands of workers, using drills, hammers and other tools right out of a home workshop.

"Not a single woman," Fancy softly observed.

"Or a married one either," Lula whispered back.

The second flick was called *Safety on the Job* and began with a quote from Lincoln: "It is the duty of every man to protect himself and those associated with him from accidents which may result in injury or death."

Lula whispered, "Maybe start by having somebody watch your back at the theater when you're in a box seat."

"Stop it," Fancy said, managing not to laugh, though she had trouble not doing so when the lights came up and the man in tan was suddenly wearing goggles, looking like he was about to drive off in a Stanley Steamer.

"Safety glasses," he explained, and took them off and whammed them on the lectern repeatedly, to show just how safe they were.

A few of the women yiped and yelped at this rowdy demonstration, but Lula just rolled her eyes at Fancy.

Finally, the man in tan turned things over to an attractive black-haired woman in a gray suit.

"I'm Head Counselor Sharon Longtin, ladies," she said, in a well-modulated alto. "I want you to know that you may bring any problems you might have to me or any of our other counselors. You'll know us because we'll be the only women wearing skirts around the production line."

Counselor Longtin then briefly discussed "women matters," including the need for a doctor's permission to work while pregnant.

"The *re*-production line," Lula cracked a little too loud for where they were seated.

Fancy laughed, and got a look from Longtin, although not a cross one. In fact, the woman just smiled and nodded a little. Fancy nodded back.

"Lockhart also enforces a strict no dating on the job policy," the counselor said. "That doesn't mean dating men who work here is forbidden. Just don't make arrangements to do so on company time. And don't take your lunch break in a supply closet getting to know a male co-worker better."

That got a few giggles from the younger girls.

"You are not to wear wristwatches, pendant earrings, necklaces, bracelets or rings. No loose sleeves, frills, nothing with cuffs or lapels. Your natural beauty will have to suffice."

That got genuine laughs.

The group was dismissed and reminded to be back for the start of their four p.m. to midnight shift, allowing an hour to get through inspection at the gate. Lula suggested they grab lunch somewhere and Fancy offered to drive.

They wound up at a little diner where the lunch crowd was just thinning out. In a booth, with Glenn Miller's "Don't Sit Under the Apple Tree" playing on the jukebox, Fancy feasted on an egg salad sandwich and Coke while Lula had a tuna salad sandwich and Green River. They shared an order of fries.

Ducking questions about herself, Fancy worked at getting Lula talking. Was that a little tinge of Texas Fancy detected?

"Guilty as charged. Grew up there. One of ten kiddies."

"Ten!"

Lula nodded, nibbled white-bread-swaddled tuna salad. "Mama always had one baby in her arms and another on the way. Really only was one thing that Papa was any good at. He got gassed by the Germans in the last war, and loud noises always set him off."

"Could he work?"

"Some. We all of us farmed – anywhere we could trade work for a shack to live in. Papa worked for the railroad a while. We had the upstairs of a nice house, for just two bucks a month, as long as we kept the place up and worked the garden. Then the Depression hit and we wound up picking cotton, Papa and us kids too. Paid us by the sack."

"I can't imagine," Fancy said, and she really couldn't.

"Finally Mama took us and moved to town. She only knew how to do one thing, really, if you know what I mean."

"I don't."

"Well...let's just say she finally figured out how to have fun without havin' kids. One fella after another come into our little apartment, mostly much younger than her, and all of a sudden money wasn't so short. Papa come around one time with a shotgun, threatening her, so one night she packed all of us kids in her car, somehow. Next I knew, I woke up in Oklahoma, which I wouldn't wish on Hitler.... I could use another Green River. Want another Coke?"

"No, I'm fine."

Lula called out to a waitress for a fresh soda.

"Anyway, eventually I wound up out here," she said, dragging a fry through ketchup. "I was a cute kid, still am far as that goes, and getting jobs like the bowling alley and drive-in and gas station was never a stretch for me. What about you, Franny?"

"What about me?"

Lula grinned. "What's a girl who comes from money doing at a defense plant? You got a guy overseas? You sure ain't chasin' sixty-some cents an hour."

"I've had it easy," Fancy admitted, embarrassed but not ashamed, "my pop having his own business and all. The Depression didn't hit us so hard. I know I'm lucky. Am I...flaunting it? I don't mean to."

"Well, a pink convertible. Kinda strings it takes to land a C sticker? Man! And those coveralls didn't come out of a Sears Roebuck catalog."

Like the fake town the aircraft plant wore, the coveralls had been made by Paramount, specifically her father's friend Edith Head, and Fancy was starting to realize how little she knew about going undercover.

Back at the Lockhart parking lot, Fancy pulled into a spot in the sea of vehicles, climbed out, and reached in back for the duffel bag. She got out the tool belt she'd been provided and slung it on. This opened Lula's eyes wider than the convertible had.

"Wow," Lula said. "Makes *my* couple of tools from home look like kid stuff."

"Well," Fancy said, the array of whatchamacallits clanking a little, "when I applied at the employment bureau, I heard you had to provide your own tools." That was accurate, except for where she'd got the info.

"You *are* a rich girl," Lula said admiringly.

"Don't spread it around."

"Honey, you're the one spreading it."

More and more, Fancy was wondering if she'd already blown this job.

Lula had left her lunch box in Fancy's car and now Fancy got hers out of the duffel, as well as the steel-toed work boots she'd been told to bring along. She traded her heels for these, then left the duffel behind as they trudged off toward their first day of work. Night of work.

Once through the rigamarole at the gate, they were greeted by a clipboard-equipped young woman in a floral long-sleeve blouse and navy slacks.

"I'm Miss Simmons," the woman said, leading them across the grounds. "Secretary to the assistant of B-24 production. I'll show you to your department."

Under a non-sky of camouflage netting, the little trio moved past dull green buildings whose roofs wore those little Hollywood-constructed faux houses and trees and streets. In the odd shadows, they passed an outdoor stage draped with a "Work to Win" banner, then a bus stop, tool store, infirmary.

"It's a city," Lula said, eyes wide, "with the neighborhoods on top."

Soon they were at an imposing structure wearing a big "4," one of its huge rolling doors humming electrically as it raised as they passed, large enough to accommodate a finished plane. They might have taken a shortcut through, but Miss Simmons took them around to the entrance. Before going in, Fancy put on her ear plugs, prepared for what was to come.

Only she wasn't.

Fancy Anders, in her short life, had been places rare for a woman of any age, including assorted continents and various great cities.

But what ocean liner's foghorn could compare to the torturous noise level of this screeching mechanical cacophony? Which high-ceilinged cathedral of Europe might outdo this vast open building of three or was it *four* towering stories? What was the brightness of a Cairo sun at noon compared to thousands of brilliant white lights flying in strict formation, kept in line by a network of steel? How could snowy alpine skiing slopes stack up against the chill of this windowless chamber, where condensation dripped like cold rain?

And how could the crowd at the Harvard/Yale football game compete with this horde of hustling, bustling workers?

And though she was a pilot herself, Fancy felt as though she'd never really seen an aircraft before, not confronted by rows of B-24 bombers lined up in various stages of completion, the tail of one nearly touching the wing of the next.

Attending each craft was the equivalent of the Grimms' fairy tale shoemaker's elves, teams of women working on high platforms under wings, and low ones under bellies. Here a ladder rose into the underside of a bomber's tail, another in front going up into the nose. There on top of the fuselage they walked and worked, as if that were a normal way to behave.

As Fancy and Lula followed their guide down the center aisle, they took it all in, though barely keeping up. Now and then they had to dodge a bicycle or small truck, and Lula almost walked into a hook lowered on a crane (someone politely yelled, "Get the hell out of the way!").

Miss Simmons said, "You'll get started right off the bat, but won't really get to meet the girls on your team till the first smoke break."

It was interesting how the secretary could get her voice up enough to be heard without screaming.

She was saying, "I should warn you, girls. You're replacing two well-liked team members. One was a school teacher, just here for the summer. But the other, a popular girl, died under...unfortunate circumstances."

Lula yelled, "An accidental death?"

"Yes. We have very few of those, but it does happen. There are dangers in a plant like this."

That much Fancy already knew.

She was here, after all, to determine whether that death really was accidental.

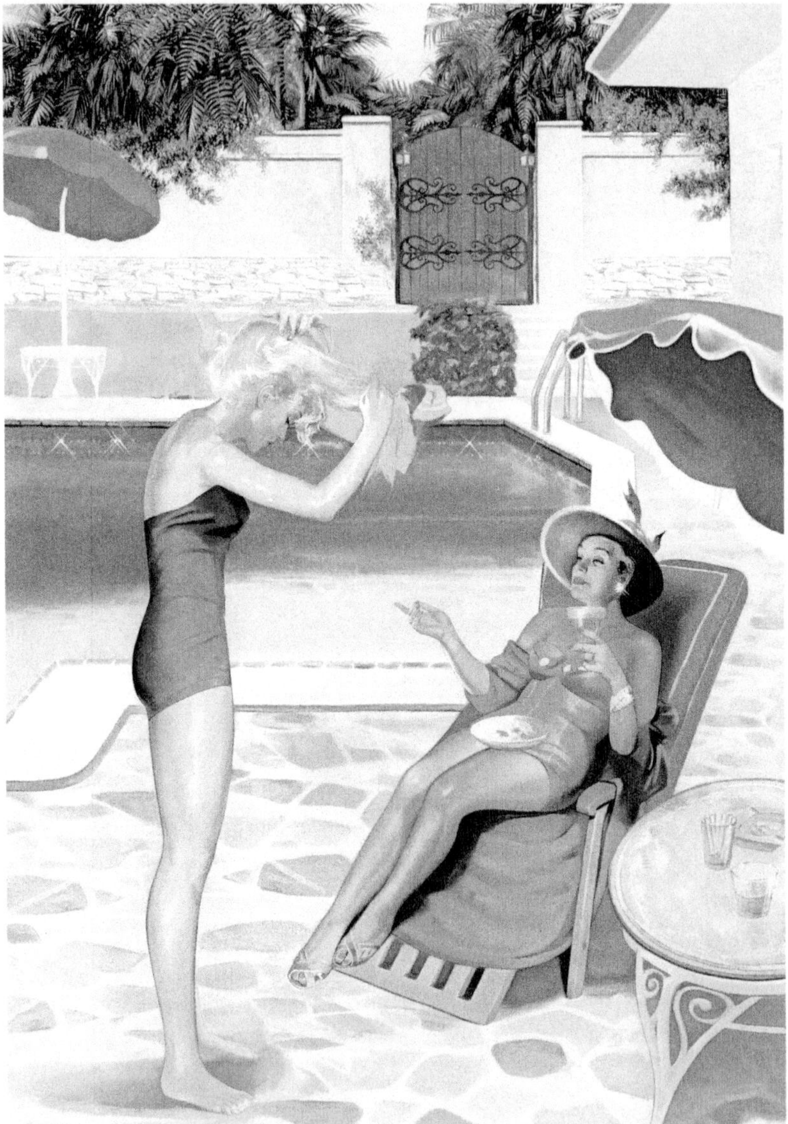

2
LONELY AT THE TOP

Francine Elizabeth Anders had long dreamed of the day she might take over her father's detective agency, but this was *not* what she had in mind.

Not that she'd ever daydreamed about her father passing away someday and leaving the business to her or anything – she adored the man! The idea of a world without Major Andrew J. Anders was practically unthinkable.

No, her fantasy that he would one day settle into a well-deserved retirement and, seeing how well his daughter had done as his secretary (a job she fully intended to expand into much more over the coming years), the reins of Anders Confidential Inquiries would be turned over to her.

Getting Daddy to give her the secretarial job had been a greater feat than when she came in third on the Bendix Trophy Race in '39, a rare accomplishment for a female pilot her age. Of course, Daddy hadn't been the obstacle, had he?

Right now she was sitting behind her father's big mahogany desk in his private office in the Bradbury Building, staring at her mother's lovely serene face in its frilly gold frame just beyond the blotter.

Charlotte Jane Anders (née Caine), sister of the publisher of *The*

Los Angeles Times, queen of the Pasadena WASPs, was a woman born wealthy with the expected snobbish attitudes but (even her daughter had to admit) a laudable interest in fundraising for various charities. The story of how her father had rescued her mother from a kidnapper and gone on to steal her heart away was the stuff dreams (and Sunday supplement articles) were made of.

Lovely Charlotte Caine, despite parental objections, had married dashing Andy Anders – eloping, of all things, something that seemed to their only child terribly out of character. But Daddy hadn't married for money, no matter what his in-laws thought – at thirty-seven, he was already a self-made man who'd built upon his experiences as an officer in the Great War and then a police detective to establish one of L.A.'s top private investigation agencies, numbering among his clients film studios, insurance firms and oil interests.

Her father adored her mother, and vice versa, and the only real conflict in their married life (Fancy well knew) was their willful daughter. She'd always been a daddy's girl, the word "tomboy" often whispered, and her mother absolutely abhorred Fancy's penchant for wearing short sleeves, slacks and slingback shoes suitable only for the likes of Katharine Hepburn and Marlene Dietrich.

Fancy had humored her mother by playing debutante in the expected gowns, landing herself properly in the society pages of the *Times*. But she and her mother were never really close, not with Fancy's penchant for such hoyden hobbies as sporty cars, motorcycles, sailboats, and planes, not to mention unchaperoned travel.

Right now what Fancy liked most about her mother was that the woman was out of town – spending the summer with Fancy's Aunt Helen in Rhode Island.

The happiest time of Fancy's young life had been the years away from her mother – though that had meant less time with her father, as well. Still, it was an acceptable trade-off, attending Barnard back east, in pursuit of a worthless major in English Literature while minoring in boys at nearby Columbia. She lost her virginity long before gaining her college degree, and fell into a rather carefree lifestyle that would have horrified her mother – smoking, drinking, running wild with girls from similarly constrained rich backgrounds.

Her father knew of such frolics, or at least suspected. But it had worked out well, really, despite a rocky start with a chilly conversation with her mother poolside in Pasadena.

Mother and daughter looked as much alike physically as they were different in every other way. Charlotte Anders had never allowed herself to gain weight, and while too much sun had taken a certain toll, she remained movie-star beautiful, having Fancy's blue eyes and high cheekbones. Or rather Fancy had hers.

Her mother lounged on a deck chair in a bathing suit of a modesty rivaling something out of the 1920s. Rarely did she ever get into the pool. Fancy, who swam all the time, was toweling off her long blonde hair, much of her physique on display in a purple Jantzen "Petty Girl" swimsuit.

As the daughter took a deck chair, her mother said, "How nice to have you around the house again."

The Barnard girl had only recently got back home.

"It's swell being here."

"What do you have in mind for yourself, dear? There's not much you can do with an English Literature degree."

Fancy thought, *Then why did you recommend one?*

But said, "No, not terribly practical, unless I want to teach. And I don't."

"Of course you don't," her mother said with a shudder. Then she turned her smile on her daughter; it was a blindingly white, vaguely threatening thing framed by a red-rouged mouth in well-tanned flesh. Her mother's eyes were very much like the ones Fancy saw in the mirror. "What, then?"

"Well," Fancy said, carefully, "I plan to talk to Daddy about my prospects."

"What prospects would those be, dear?"

"I'd like to go to work for him." As an investigator, but she said, "Something administrative around the office."

"Out of the question. You and I have things to do. Places to go. People to see."

Charitable events, fancy dress balls, weddings, mother-daughter world cruises – with the only goal, Fancy knew, *of ferreting out a man of proper social standing worthy of the niece of L.A.'s most powerful newspaper publisher.*

"We'll have to talk," Fancy said, pleasantly, heading off any confrontation and padding inside, still drying her hair.

She had known not to talk to her father at home about it, not even in the privacy of his study. Instead she dropped in at his office just before lunch and cajoled him into taking her to the Brown Derby for a Cobb Salad.

Her father, who had not a lick of pretension about him, ordered a burger as the duo shared a booth. He had always reminded her of the actor Melvyn Douglas, the same strong, masculine features with that jaunty mustache giving him a touch of sophistication – impeccable in a lightweight gray herringbone suit courtesy of Adrian at MGM.

As they had coffee after the meal, she said, "I want to join the family business."

"What, journalism? Columnist or some such thing? I suppose your schooling prepared you for that."

"No. *Your* business. I'd like to train as an investigator, but will do anything from cleaning up to filing to...*anything*, Daddy."

His expression somehow mingled amusement and terror. "Your mother would not be pleased."

"I know. But I'm not going to spend my life trying to please her."

"So I've gathered. Are you trying to please me?"

"Not even that. Give me a chance."

He pulled a breath in and let it out slowly. "I can use a secretary. I just lost Penny, as you know. And I could arrange a crash course at a secretarial college."

"Yes. Fine. That would be super!"

Her mother's response to this was not to speak to Daddy for a week and Fancy for a month. Her first perk!

Fancy, already an accomplished typist, took a week's training with ease, then learned shorthand in her spare time. She got to know all sixteen of the operatives in the bullpen, and paid attention to the work being done by the older woman who was her father's administrative assistant. Her father was obviously pleased. The future bode well.

Then, not long after the Japanese attack on Pearl Harbor, he called her in to his private office, where she stood at the ready with her pad and pen.

"You won't be needing that, darling," he told her. "Sit. Please."

Something was wrong – he never spoke to her in affectionate terms at work, even with no one else around.

"I've been called back to military service," he said. "Specifically, I'll be working with my old friend Bill Donovan to put together the Office of Strategic Services."

"What kind of office is that?"

He thought a moment before answering. "Military intelligence. I'll be working out of D.C., but could go overseas at any time. And if that happens...really, *when* that happens...you and your mother will not know where I'm stationed. It will be Top Secret."

She felt at once proud and devastated.

She flew from the chair and went to him and he rose. They embraced. Then still in his arms, she said, "I'll hold down the fort. I'm up to it. I really am. And I'll be good to Mother."

He hugged her and shooed her back to her chair.

"Listen, kiddo," he said, "I have to admit something to you. I was in favor of you working here in hopes I could...don't take this wrong. Straighten you out."

"Why, was I so badly bent?"

He twitched a smile. "I'm a detective, honey. I notice things. Do you think I wasn't keeping an eye on you at that college? Do you think I didn't know about your...hedonistic ways? Well, I wanted you to grow out of that, and you have."

And she guessed he was right – she'd stopped smoking, hardly ever imbibed, and only went out on Saturday nights.

"You're already the best secretary I ever had," he told her, "and now I'm going to put you in charge around here."

"Daddy! You won't regret it."

"Don't be so sure *you* won't. I'm largely shutting the agency down for the duration. We only have four operatives who haven't already enlisted, and I'll get them situated elsewhere. Your job will be to sit by the phone and make referrals to other agencies. I don't want to use an answering service – you doing it will lend the personal touch. You'll do the mail, keep the files up to date, and...spruce the place up. You know, just a little light dusting and so on. After all, you did volunteer for that."

She nodded. She put on a brave face. What lay ahead for her father left no room for her to be anything but a good solider.

So now she sat at his desk in the private office whose glassed-in front wall looked out onto the sixteen empty desks that she regularly dusted. The walls around her were arrayed with photos of her father from his Great War days to his police years, and on to more recent times as he posed with movie stars and political figures. Awards, diplomas, commendations and licenses were framed as well, lurking above wooden file cabinets. Traffic sounds were lighter since gas rationing, and she spent much of her time listening to the radio (*Backstage Wife*) or reading (*Kitty Foyle*) or doing her exercises (push-ups, sit-ups, jumping jacks). The phone rang so seldom it *really* made her jump.

Like it did right now.

"Anders Confidential Inquiries," she told the phone.

"Fancy, it's Rick."

Lt. Rick Hinder, LAPD, was the liaison between the various police departments in the greater Los Angeles area; a new position, anticipating a greater wartime need for such cooperation.

"What can I do for you, Lieutenant?"

"This isn't me asking for a date."

"Good. Because I'm not interested."

"This is police business. Or, anyway, it's potentially police business."

"I'm listening."

"I'm looking into something for Douglas Lockhart. He's a friend of your father's, I understand. And you know him, right?"

Douglas R. Lockhart, 50, was president of Amalgamated Aircraft. In the early 1920s, he designed the first plane with a payload greater than its own weight. From that early success, Lockhart had merged his small company with two major ones and was now one of the most respected and successful aeronautic engineers and industrialists in America. Fancy had known him since childhood.

"We've met," she said.

"Listen, I damn well realize you're essentially shut down over there, but I think you might be able to steer Lockhart in the right direction. Can I bring him over there for a consult?"

She kept the spike of interest out of her voice. "I think I can find time."

"Come on, Fancy. Last time I stopped by you were hoovering the floor. We'll be over this afternoon. Two all right?"

"Two's fine."

She hung up without saying goodbye. Hinder irritated her. He was a no-good, good-looking son of a bitch with a wife and kid but kept asking her out anyway. True, he and his missus were separated, but...worse yet, he looked like Tyrone Power.

One nice thing about having money was that she could afford to buy something nice to wear when something unexpected came up. Fancy walked to the May Company's store at Eighth and Broadway and bought herself a smart man-tailored gray suit – blouse and slacks just wouldn't do for a meeting with the president of an aircraft company.

When the buzzer came, she went out and opened the door and Lockhart stepped in first. The industrialist – stocky with a high forehead, graying brown hair and friendly squinty features – wore a homburg and dark-gray pinstripe suit and carried a leather briefcase. The fedora-sporting Rick closed the door behind them as Lockhart came over and gave her a big hug.

"Uncle Doug," she said. "So good to see you."

That familiarity got Rick's eyes popping.

"You're the image of your mother," Lockhart said, taking off the homburg, "but somehow you take after your father, too."

They stood chatting about his wife, kids and grandkids – he was not her real uncle, just an old family friend – while handsome Rick just looked on, awkward in his off-the-rack dark brown suit. Honest cops couldn't afford better, and dishonest ones knew enough not to.

In her father's inner sanctum, she got behind the desk, Lockhart took the client's chair, and Rick just milled. He obviously hadn't been aware of how well Fancy and the aircraft tycoon knew each another.

Lockhart asked, "What do you hear from your old man?"

"Not much. He's still in D.C. That's really all I know, except he misses Mother and me."

"Great man, your father."

"He's okay," she admitted with a smile.

Rick, who was turning his hat around in his hands like pizza dough, leaned in and said, "Mr. Lockhart is wondering if you might know of someone who could do a job for him."

Had Rick brought Lockhart around simply as an excuse to take another amorous crack at her? Obviously a police detective knew all sorts of people to recommend as investigators, since almost all P.I.s were ex-cops.

Lockhart said, "It's a very specific kind of operative we need, Fancy. You'll be paid for your referral."

She waved that off. "That's not necessary. Really."

"Actually it is. This is a confidential matter and we'll need your agency on retainer to make it official. As I recall, your father issues all contracts through an attorney, to maintain a client privacy privilege?"

"That's right," she said, a little confused now.

Lockhart placed the briefcase on the desk, snapped it open, took some manila folders out and asked if he might come around and show her something and she said of course. He plopped several folders before her, flipped the top one open.

A color poster depicted an attractive but determined woman with a polka-dot babushka; she was making a muscle, saying (via a comic-strip word balloon), "WE CAN DO IT!"

Lockhart slid that poster aside and revealed one showing a woman in a red snood using a drill on a girder: "Do the Job HE Left Behind!" Similar images of women war workers followed – "The More Women at WORK, the Sooner We Win!" and "Women in the War – We Can't Win Without Them!"

"These are prototypes," Lockhart said, leaning in next to her, "representing a major propaganda push to encourage women to take jobs in shipyards, munitions factories...and aircraft plants like mine."

"This is your project, Uncle Doug?"

"I'm part of it."

Rick put in: "A major part."

Lockhart said, "I'm working with the Office of War Information. The idea is to create an image that will become as familiar as Mickey Mouse or Uncle Sam – a woman clad in overalls handling tools with the ease of any man."

"These are all artist's representations," she said. "It's effective, but—"

"You're ahead of me, Fancy."

He gathered the sample posters and moved onto the next folder. This he flipped open and began showing her a succession of shots of a beautiful young woman, as blonde as Fancy herself, actually working in an aircraft plant. Though each photo was as carefully staged as a pin-up, and as alluring, the reality of the setting, as this girl stood on a platform wielding a rivet gun, was unmistakable.

"This is Rose Hannold," Lockhart said. "An employee at our Long Beach plant."

"She's lovely."

"She was."

"Was?"

His expression grew grave. "We had big plans for her – 'Rosie the Riveter,' we were going to call her. We even commissioned a song about her. Norman Rockwell agreed to do a painting for the *Saturday Evening Post*. We were ready to go full-speed ahead with Rose as the star of our publicity campaign. But a platform she was working on gave way and she took a tumble – a fatal one."

Rick said, "The Long Beach police looked into it and the inquest called it an accident."

"But I have my doubts," Lockhart said. "She was working the night shift. Called me from there and wanted to meet the next day. She didn't say about what, but she was clearly upset. I got the sense she might be in danger."

Rick said, "It's not officially a police matter anymore, and there's not enough for the FBI. We want to send a girl in undercover to look into it. The couple of ex-policewomen I know aren't working for any agencies."

Lockhart said, "We were hoping maybe you might be able to think of somebody to recommend."

"I think I have just the one," Fancy said.

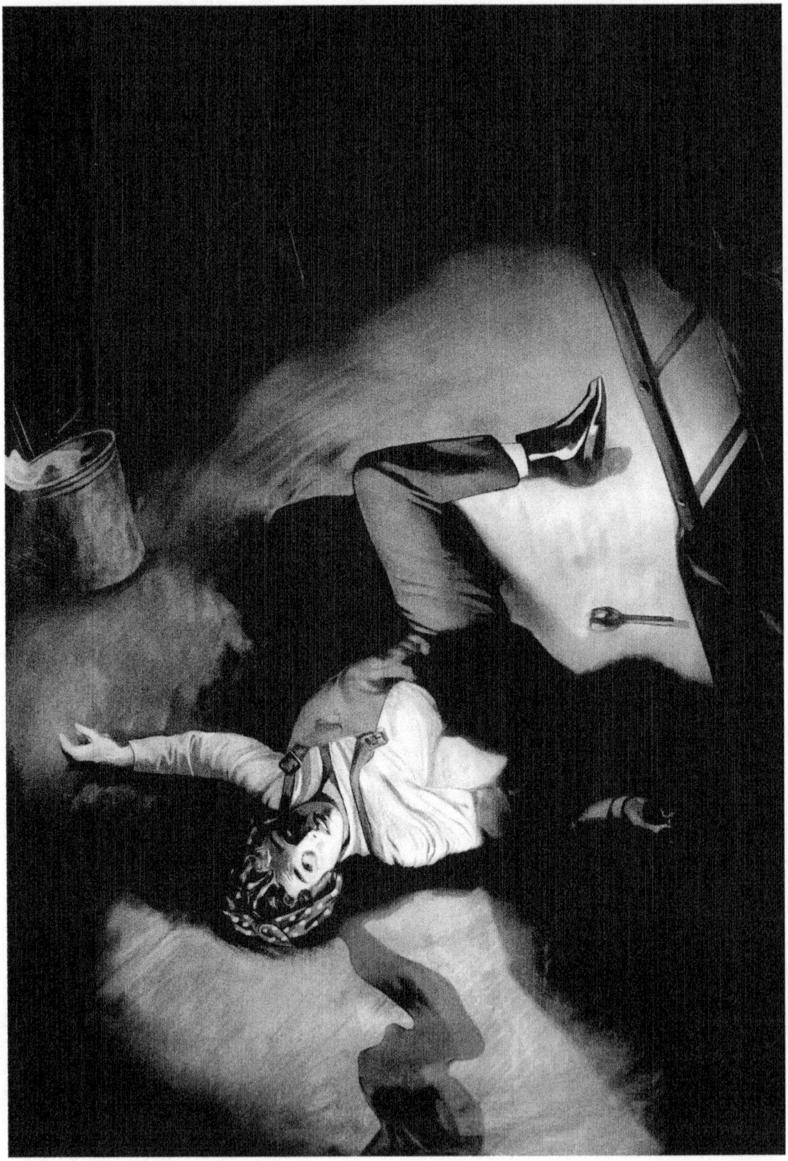

3

NEW FRIENDS AND AN OLD ONE

Miss Simmons, with Fancy on her right and Lula on her left, moved down the center aisle of Building Four along which occasional stairs rose to open offices on expansive platforms, under which first-aid stations were doing their good work. Time clocks affixed to steel beams popped up now and then like stubborn mushrooms.

Their escort nodded toward one of these, telling Fancy and Lula this was where, after today, they would be punching in. They'd already punched in elsewhere, so were in no danger of being short-changed, no matter how worthless Fancy figured they might be on their first day.

"The numbers on the girders above the ships," Miss Simmons said, "tell you how to locate your position on the line."

Lula, having to yell, asked, "Ships?"

Miss Simmons had the art of talking loud but naturally down pat. "Yes, ships, *not* planes. You don't want to get the terminology wrong, or they'll never let you forget it."

Fancy asked, "Who won't?"

"The men."

And there *were* a fair number of men at work here. That queue of women outside had led Fancy to believe this would be an all-female workplace, as had Douglas Lockhart's propaganda pieces. Certainly the women outnumbered the men, but males were on hand, all right. And Fancy noted only two distinct male reactions as she and Lula were ushered along – wolf-whistle leers and sour disgust.

Neither reaction applied to the short, crusty-looking gent in a blue shirt with a red badge who was approaching from the opposite direction. His hair was white and short and yet unruly, like tumbleweed; his face was weathered and lined, his features distorted by an unforgiving middle age, but his eyes were a light blue as pretty as Fancy's.

When he caught up to them, Miss Simmons said, "Mr. Burrows, this is Miss Franny Allison and Miss Lula Hall. Ladies, this is Mr. Hank Burrows, your foreman. I'll leave you with him."

And she was gone.

Burrows walked them over to one side, as if wanting to get closer to the rat-a-tat-tat of a rivet gun. He stood in front of Fancy and looked at her hips; she was just starting to get annoyed when he said, "Nice tool belt, daughter. Where'd you get that?"

"My uncle," she said. Sort of true.

"He knows his stuff, your uncle." The rough-looking little man moved on to Lula. "No tool belt or kit?"

"No, sir."

"Weren't you told to bring tools from home?"

"Yes, sir. But this is all we had around."

Lula opened her lunch box and a hammer and screw driver were on either side of an apple and a wax-papered sandwich, the tools nestling where a Thermos might be.

"You need a box or a belt," he said, frowning, "and the tools on that list they give you."

"Yes, sir."

"And don't call me 'sir.' I'm Mr. Burrows and maybe 'Hank,' if you get yourself the right tools and I take a shine to you. Understand, daughter?"

Fancy realized now that as key as his own name was to him, Mr. Burrows would not be bothering with learning theirs – all females were apparently "daughter."

He walked them back out into the center aisle, as noise and work went on around them, seeming somehow at once frantic and methodical.

He said, "I need to warn you girls about one thing."

Just one? Fancy wondered.

"We take all kinds here at Amalgamated. There's a war on, you know."

Somehow both young women managed to let that straight line go unanswered.

The foreman was saying, "We got colored here and Mexies and various kinds of you females, all doin' their part, and we don't truck with no prejudicial nonsense."

"Good to know," Fancy said, the sarcasm not showing.

"Doesn't bother me," Lula said, with a shrug as they walked along at a good clip. "My grandmother's a full-blooded Cherokee. On my mother's side."

The foreman had no response to that, though his frown indicated he might have been trying to process one. Fancy was thinking how Lula continued to be full of surprises.

Finally they were at Department 190, as the number on a girder confirmed, where Fancy was at once struck by how the women workers were displaying strength and agility that might be envied by any of those men's men who were either horny having them around or unhappy about it. These "girls" were scaling ladders and wriggling into tight spaces to reach impossible places that needed drilling or riveting.

And Fancy indeed saw various skin tones that didn't qualify as Caucasian, but also an age variance she hadn't expected – the several teams working here at once ranged from late teens well into the fifties, perhaps sixties.

Burrows gathered his two charges for one last little speech. "Daughters, you may be here on a lark, you may be here to make better money than waitin' tables, you may even be here 'cause you're good American girls. But I got a brother flying one of these babies..." He jerked at thumb at the looming B-24 being built. "...and I want him to come home in one piece. So make sure every ship flies right and true.... This here is Mr. Joe Dawson, your leadman. You'll be seein' a lot more of him than me."

A husky, muscular guy with cropped brown hair and a cocky smile ambled up, wiping his hands with a rag; he had a yellow badge, too, but his read LEADMAN along one side. Fancy guessed Joe Dawson was what people meant by "ruggedly handsome," though his squinty dark eyes spoiled it a bit. Still, he filled out the brown khaki jumpsuit well enough. Foreman Burrows made the introductions and then the plant swallowed him up, too, without so much as a burp.

"Would you ladies like the nickel tour?" Dawson asked in the near yell they would all soon assume. His smirk might make some girls swoon, but Fancy would just as soon have slapped him. But she'd make an effort to get along.

They took the tour, following the leadman up a ladder into the tail section, where the world became a gleaming metal one – it was like being inside a prairie schooner made of tin. They moved around and sometimes over women working, with Dawson motioning nonchalantly at one thing or another, explaining quickly what each item did – this was a bulkhead, that was a belt frame – in a way that Fancy felt was less to inform and more to show off.

Even if she'd been able to comprehend any of it, the cursory explanations were compromised by the rattling riveting going on in the tail by a woman behind them. Ahead a rare male was adjusting some overhead pipes while a female was sticking a clump of wires through a hole above a window.

When Fancy walked by that window, she had a woozy moment, as the outside world seemed at an angle.

Dawson led them up into the fore of the ship. *This is where the belly turret goes. That's where the life raft is stored. This is the command deck.* Following him as he crouched to access a small door onto a catwalk, they heard him say, "Bomb bay's here." This he told them as they aped his movement, going sideways between opposing racks, stepping over motors, boxes and cans littering the catwalk.

Toward the front of the bomb bay, he told them, was the underflight deck. Soon he got them up to the flight deck, where the pilot and radio man and navigator had specific seats.

When they'd climbed down out of B-24, Dawson asked the two newcomers if they had any questions and, as if in response, a whistle blew like a colossal Bronx cheer.

Fancy stifled a laugh but Lula didn't bother.

Work ceased and a small army of women and a handful of men crawled down from, and out of, the in-progress B-24 like ants heading for a picnic. Same was true of those working on other B-24s all around.

Lula asked Dawson, "Is it mealtime already?"

"Just the 6:30 smoke break," Dawson said. "Hey, you girls on the first team! Come over here."

Four women fell into a group, frowning in tandem at having their precious break time intruded upon; but they came over just the same.

Dawson singled them out with hand flips. "That's Ethel Walsh," he said, indicating a lanky, weathered woman of maybe fifty in coveralls a little too big for her.

"Howdy," Ethel said.

"Colored gal," Dawson continued, "is Maggie Mae King."

"Negro, y'don't mind," said the handsome woman with no

apparent rancor, or respect for that matter. Her head was covered with a red-and-black bandanna and she filled her coveralls out voluptuously.

"I don't mind, honey," Dawson said. "And Little Miss Zoot Suit there is Carmen Something."

"*Cervantes*," the girl corrected, an irritated frown on her bright red-lipsticked mouth, her high black pompadour in a heavy white cotton hairnet. Pretty and probably still in her teens, Carmen was indeed wearing a Zoot-suit-style fingertip coat over jeans with rolled-up cuffs.

"These are your new teammates," Dawson said. "Franny Allison and Lula Hall." Then he tactlessly added, "Try to bring 'em back alive."

As he started to go, the foreman patted Fancy on the fanny and turned toward the aisle, waiting for a small truck to pass. Fancy patted him back the same way – harder. He looked over his shoulder, startled, then fake laughed and was off.

But Fancy's gesture had already won over the rest of the women, because they were laughing, quite genuinely, and slipping arms around each other. The two new girls shook hands with the three old pros, who showed them the way to the field, where they could sit and smoke or have a snack while they appraised the B-24s lined up there as if for the team's own proud inspection.

All three of the veteran members smoked, and eagerly; Lula lighted up, as well. But Fancy had not been lying to her father when she said she'd given up smoking, and she just sat on the grass, her knees up, snugged with her hands. She asked, "You girls take all your smoke breaks out here?"

Maggie Mae shook her head. "Just this first one, 'cause it's still sunny out and usually nice and cool. We stay inside for the eleven break. Just sit along the aisle and on platforms and ladders and what have you."

Lula asked, "What's the story on that Dawson dope, anyway?"

"He's just full of himself," Carmen said, shrugging. "God's gift. Got a yen for empennage."

Fancy asked, "What's that?"

"Tail assemblies. It's what these letches call a woman's backside."

"That old boy Burrows," Ethel chimed in, "is the one to *really* watch."

Lula laughed. "You're kidding!"

"No she isn't," Carmen said. "That old coot has more hands than a box of clocks. When he calls me 'daughter,' it makes my skin crawl."

"Aw, he's harmless," Maggie Mae said. "Case of assault with a dead weapon."

That got a round of laughs.

Fancy asked, "So, where's everybody from?"

"Compton," Maggie Mae said.

"Eastside L.A.," Carmen said. "Ethel's from Kansas. Hey, Ethel, tell 'em about the rattlesnake!"

"Nobody cares about the rattlesnake," Ethel said.

But they all, Fancy and Lula included, cheered her on.

"It's not a story," Ethel insisted. "I was just a tike when we lit out from Kansas in a covered wagon..."

Fancy thought, *Not one made of tin, either!*

"...takin' what food along we could. No way to buy any, between bein' broke and with no place to buy some. When we run out, my brothers would go out and shoot prairie chickens. One time they couldn't find any, so they killed this big rattlesnake and made steaks out of it. Delicious! But when Papa cleaned the snake, he give me the rattle to play with. I played with that rattle for years. Told you it wasn't a story."

Fancy asked, "How did you wind up out here, Ethel?"

"Well, my husband Ed and me lost our farm in the Depression. We picked apples in Colorado for a while. Then went back to Kansas and picked berries. Twenty-five cents an hour. We come to Long

Beach for something better. Ed got a good job as a janitor in a gas station, but with rationing, it didn't last. Now Ed works here, too. Building Three. We take different shifts so there's somebody to look after the three boys still at home. One son's in the Air Force. Partly why I'm here."

Fancy had always known that she'd been lucky being born to Andrew and Charlotte Anders. But she never truly knew how lucky till now.

"Where are you from, Franny?" Maggie Mae asked.

"Pasadena," Fancy admitted.

Carmen said, "I knew some folks tried to rent a place there."

"Oh?"

"Landlords won't rent to my kind."

Maggie Mae said, "Tell me about it. Least at defense plants they call *you* 'white' on the application forms."

"For all the good it does," Carmen grunted.

Things got quiet.

Then Fancy, knowing exactly what she was doing, asked, "What was that crack Dawson made? Bring 'em back alive? What's that about?"

Her three new friends exchanged troubled glances.

"We just lost two from this team," Maggie Mae said. "A real nice school teacher helpin' out for the summer. But also a sweet, pretty kid from L.A. name of Rose."

"Rose Hannold," Lula put in. "She stayed at the Studio Hotel in Hollywood where I live."

Lula never stopped surprising.

Carmen asked Lula, "You knew Rose?"

"Just a little. To say hello. We weren't roommates or anything. She came out from the Midwest to make it in the movies, I think. But she died recently, I heard."

Maggie Mae said, "Right here. On the job. Took a tumble from a platform. Busted her skull wide open. Pity, such a pretty child. Terrible thing."

Fancy asked, "You all saw this?"

"Lord sake, no," Maggie Mae said. "She was workin' through a break 'cause we was behind. Rest of us wasn't about to miss a smoke break. Only Dawson and Burrows both been pushin' her."

Literally? Fancy wondered.

Carmen said, "We liked her. She was real sweet, but…"

"But?" Lula asked.

"These men who come around, on the make? Flirting right and left?" Carmen frowned fleetingly. "Let's just say she gave as good as she got."

Fancy asked, "What do you mean by that?"

Carmen hesitated. "I don't like to speak ill of the dead…"

"Then don't," Ethel said crisply.

Carmen sighed. "She wasn't a bad girl or anything. It's just…when Burrows got handsy with her, or Dawson was putting the moves on, she let 'em get away with it."

"Didn't go anywheres," Ethel said.

"No, it didn't," Carmen said. "Golly, I didn't mean to imply that she…look, let's face it. Rose liked to play the vamp, but she didn't put out, okay?"

"That can get a gal in dutch," Maggie Mae said.

"Do you think there's anything…suspicious," Fancy asked, "about how Rose died?"

But the whistle blew again, and Fancy's question didn't get answered, as the women gathered themselves and headed back into Building Four.

Fancy stopped to use the ladies' restroom, and none of the rest of her team was around when someone called out.

"*Fancy!*"

She wheeled toward the sound, half reflex, half panic. She realized that just trying to get lost in the crowd wouldn't cover it. Instead she merely froze there with as much of a smile as she could manage plastered on her face.

Charles "Chip" Vincent was coming right at her, grinning like he'd spotted a long-lost love...and he kind of had. Chip's family – Mr. Vincent was a real estate magnate in L.A. – ran in the same rarefied circles as Fancy's. In fact, her mother had fixed her up with Chip, who was the rare rich kid the girl could stand. He was funny and fun, and thought his parents were idiots. She could relate, at least to half of it.

"What are you doing here?" he asked her. They were just outside the restroom area. She walked him over near a first-aid station.

"What are *you* doing here?" she asked him.

Chip – blond, blue-eyed, boyish, in coveralls almost as nice as hers – was a sailing aficionado, which was something else they had in common.

"I'm working here," Chip said.

She didn't know of him ever to hold a job, not even with his father's business.

"Gosh," he said, "it's great to see you. You can't be working *here!* *Are* you working here?"

"You first. What's the deal?"

"The deal is my father got me this aircraft job to justify my deferral. There. Keep the embarrassing truth to yourself. Now you."

She spoke as softly as she could in this funhouse and still be heard. "First of all, don't call me Fancy. And my last name isn't Anders."

He smirked. "*Sure* it isn't."

"It's Franny Allison. Say it."

"...Franny Allison."

"Again."

"Franny Allison, I got it, I got it. What's going on?"

She shook a finger at him. "I'm working undercover for the *Times*, doing a story about an average girl working in a defense job."

"You're about as average as Merle Oberon."

"Maybe so, but don't spoil it for me. Got it? Now I need to get back on the line. Don't you?"

He nodded, and wandered off, looking a little confused, even more so than usual, an old flame Fancy had no interest in rekindling.

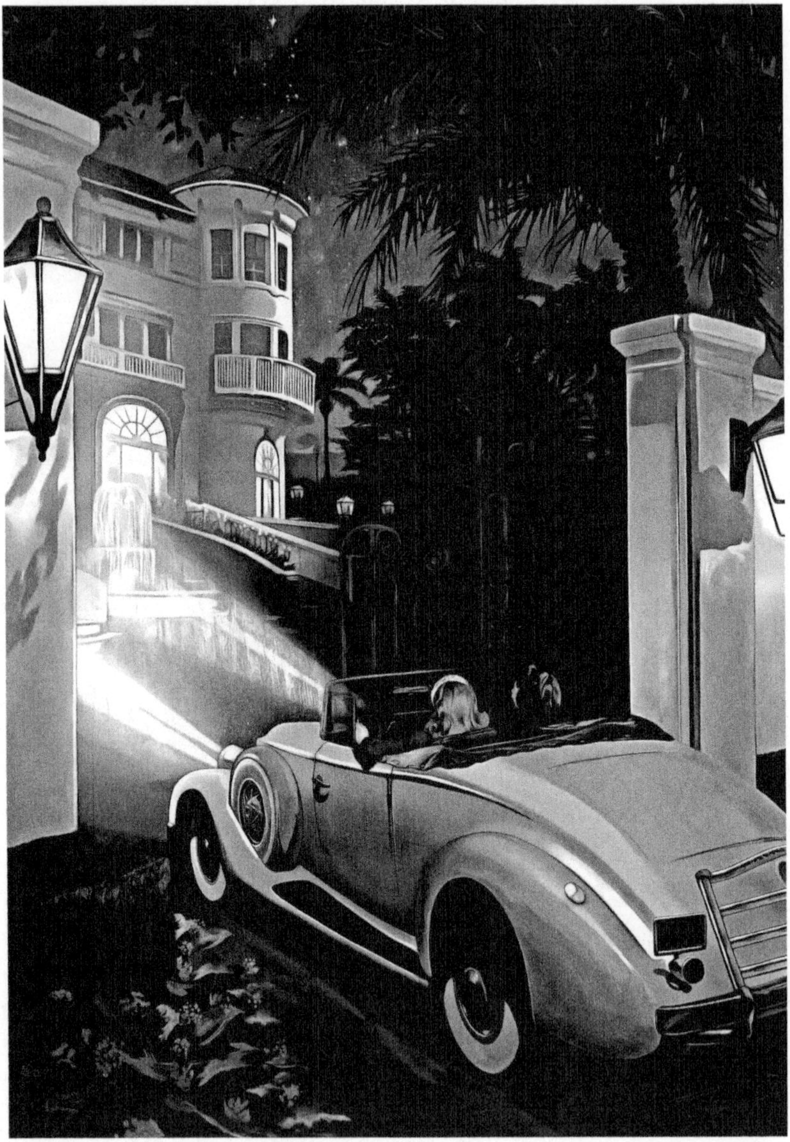

4
GIRL TALK

By the end of their first week, "Franny Allison" and Lula Hall had become quite a pair, riveting and bucking with the best of them.

A riveting gun – nicknamed a "Buck Rogers," after the funny-page spaceman's futuristic weapon, going well with the goggles both girls wore – was only six inches long, weighing three and a half pounds. Bucking bars were steel blocks of various sizes and weights, providing a solid backing to flatten to the end of the rivet while tightening it. This required more muscle than shooting rivets, even though the Buck Rogers vibrated like an earthquake in Fancy's work-gloved hands, making a racket like Spike Jones and His City Slickers falling down the stairs.

As they addressed the skin of a ship, one woman would work outside, the other in, the first inserting the rivet, the other applying strips of cheesecloth and paste across the inner seam. Then the riveter riveted and the bucker bucked. After half an hour, the two young women would trade off, one going inside the shell to buck while the other moved outside to take over the more exhausting riveting. This went on for hours.

Fancy couldn't help recalling the artist renderings of the imaginary Rosie the Riveter and photographs of the real Rose Hannold supposedly on the job, clean, well-dressed, without work gloves and with jewelry. The reality, Fancy now knew, was a grubby, sweaty one – her face smudged, hands filthy with chemicals, nails edged in black, metal shavings in her hair despite the turban. Her baby-blue coveralls bore grease streaks and a tear in one knee, and she'd bumped her shins, stubbed her toes, and knocked her head.

By the end of shift, all a girl wanted was a hot, soapy bath to soak in. Any smoke break or mealtime talk of an after-work all-night movie or making it to Long Beach's Majestic Ballroom where dancing went on into the wee hours was long forgotten. At least this first week of work that was so.

Maybe she'd get used to it; maybe it would get easier. The old pros on the team assured Fancy and Lula it would. For now, both women lumbered out of Building Four at one p.m., part of a mostly female crowd moving toward the brightly illuminated front gates. The two lugged their lunch boxes, staggering past the big black shapes of looming buildings under camouflage webbing.

The vast parking lot brimmed with workers leaving and arriving, but the lighting was barely sufficient – the area unprotected from overhead view by any netting.

"Tomorrow's Saturday," Fancy said. Her voice sounded like sandpaper in her ears.

"It's the rumor," Lula admitted.

They were at Fancy's Packard. This was where Lula regularly headed on to the bus stop.

"Why don't you pack an overnight bag," Fancy said, "and bring it to work tomorrow."

"Why? So we can head for the border?"

"You come home with me tomorrow night. Morning. Whatever you want to call it. We'll have a lazy day at my place on Sunday."

Lula stood staring at Fancy in the dim lighting, as if trying to make out something in a fuzzy photo. "Look, uh...I like you, Fran, but my gate only swings one way. We're just friends."

Fancy grinned. "Honey, I don't give a damn what two girls do together, or two boys for that matter. I've read Havelock Ellis. In these times, anyone who has time to care about such trivialities just isn't doing their bit."

"Oh. Well. Just a sleepover then?"

"Easier than having you take a bus from Hollywood. I'm going to invite Maggie Mae and Carmen to join us – not for the overnight, but a little pool party."

Lula was suspicious again. "Who's Havelock Ellis?"

Fancy laughed, even though doing so seem to hurt every fiber of her overworked body. "I like boys, okay? *Some* boys. Not foremen and leadmen, though."

Lula was smiling now. "Okay, I'll pack a bag. Stay with your car tomorrow till I show up, so I can stow it."

But the next day Lula had something on her mind. Was she still worried that Fancy had romantic intentions? That didn't seem likely. When the eight p.m. whistle blew – "lunch" in the brightly illuminated Building Four – they were both ragged from riveting and bucking. Fancy suggested they skip the lunches they'd brought and eat in the cafeteria, where the other three team members never did.

They sat facing each other across a small side table over meat loaf and mashed potatoes and Fancy said, "Are you still afraid I'm mooning over your swell body?"

Lula smiled a little. "No. It's not that."

"What is it then?"

"I noticed something when I climbed in the front seat of your car, you know...when I tossed my suitcase in the back?"

"Okay, what?"

"Your driver's registration on the steering column. Your name isn't Franny Allison, is it?"

Her first week here, and already her cover had been blown for a second time!

"No," Fancy admitted.

"Francine Anders. Kinda similar. Same initials, but..."

Fancy was about to give Lula the same line of bull as Chip Vincent, about being a reporter doing a story, blah blah blah. Then she thought better of it.

"Do you trust me, Lula?"

"Well, I *did*."

"You still can. But I don't want to go into it here. It's nothing dishonest. I'm not an Axis spy or anything. If you'll come home with me tonight, I will neither attempt to seduce you nor tie you to a rack to torture you into spilling what you know about bucking and riveting."

Lula had been drinking milk during that, and it made her laugh, and the milk came out her nose, which made Fancy laugh.

"Okay, Mata Hari," Lula said. "I'll risk a night in a comfy bed in a nice house. I *assume* it's a nice house – I mean, you really *are* rich, aren't you?"

"Yeah. Really rich."

Lula made a face. "Wish I'd known before I paid for my own lunch."

The ride up to L.A. after shift was a warm one, cooled by having the convertible's top down. That made it a little noisy for talking; but after six days of the clamor filling that hangar-like plant, both young women were old hands at speaking up by now.

Fancy spilled – held nothing back. The Rosie the Riveter propaganda campaign, Douglas Lockhart hiring her, Rick Hinder, everything.

"Well," Lula said, "you haven't had much time to do any investigating yet."

"All too true. That plant isn't a place where much casual conversation goes on, except on breaks and lunch."

"And you've skipped a couple of smoke breaks."

"Yeah, I'm not a smoker, and anyway I figure I can talk to the team on lunches. I'm really hoping to get somewhere tomorrow, when the girls relax at my place."

"It's going to be tough not to give yourself away. Are you experienced at this undercover work? Trained in it?"

"Not at all."

Lula grinned. "Well, you learned to rivet and buck in a week. What *can't* you pick up in a hurry?"

"On those smoke breaks I've struck up conversations with the women on either side and across from us. Anybody who might have seen what happened with Rose."

"I don't think anybody saw that, or anyway anybody who's admitting to it. It was Carmen who found Rose."

"Yeah. That much I got."

"But the others were right behind her. Say, you didn't ask Ethel to your pool party, huh?"

"No, she lives in Long Beach and has a husband and three boys on her hands. I figure the younger, single women would've had more to do with Rose. And I need to get close to Hank Burrows and Joe Dawson."

"*That* won't be tough."

Between the whistling wind and the purr of the motor, the pair tired of conversation. They'd had a brutal day, and Lula fell asleep before they got to Pasadena. When Fancy pulled into the drive, going a little faster than she should, that woke up her passenger, who blinked and said, "Am I dreaming?"

"No, this is the ol' homestead."

Washed in moonlight, nestled among swaying palms and mature

olive trees, the three-story Mission Revival mansion off Orange Grove Avenue suggested that maybe the wealthiest padres under a generous God's sky might reside there.

Lula was sitting up on her side of the Packard. "I may have to revise my idea of 'rich.'"

"Disappointed?"

"Yeah. I was expecting something really grand."

Embarrassed by her family's opulence, Fancy said, "It's only six bedrooms and five baths."

"Don't. Just don't."

In the rotunda entry, with Lula lugging her bag in, and both girls still in their work clothes, Fancy felt painfully awkward. She said, "Are you...irritated with me?"

"No. I'm just thinking about taking back my remark about not swinging both ways. I'm ready to marry you."

They both laughed, and it echoed, then they stepped into the living room. A staircase with a wrought-iron banister was in front of them, and modern furnishings in the Art Deco style were tastefully arranged; French doors looked onto a patio, and over a carved plaster fireplace hung a Picasso depicting a woman in a geometric manner, clearly confusing Lula, who gave Fancy a look that said, *Couldn't you people afford something better?*

Then Lula put her bag down and said, "I want a tour. Not a nickel tour like that dope Dawson gave us of our B-24, but the quarter tour. I want the works."

Fancy didn't argue. She dutifully escorted her friend through the dining room, bedrooms, bathrooms, office, wine cellar, library and more, the magnesite flooring, wrought-iron railings, plaster moldings, and stained-glass windows. Thankfully Lula was too tired to ask many questions, or was maybe just too overwhelmed.

They wound up in the big white kitchen, which was every bit as modern looking as a Buck Rogers rivet gun only sleeker. They had beers, Hamm's, her father's favorite and one of many banes of her mother's existence. But Fancy and Lula were working girls and the bottled brew from the Land of Sky Blue Waters was just the thing.

Lula was staring into nothing as she took swigs. "I worked in a mansion when I was thirteen. They had rugs and a radio and everything. Washed for those people, ironed, cooked, sewed. Six months they worked me like a dog, day and night. I quit. Anyway...I *thought* it was a mansion."

"Why don't you move in here with me for a while?"

"What?"

"We can drive to work together. My mother's away for God knows how long, and my dad's in D.C. The help is just a cook and my father's assistant, the butler really, but Daddy won't let Mother call him that."

"I do," Lula said solemnly.

"You do what?"

"Take you for my lawful wedded husband."

They both laughed, really laughed, though it had only been one beer. But it had been a hell of a long day.

The team, all but Ethel, sat along one side of the pool in deck chairs. Carmen couldn't have looked cuter with her high pompadour unnetted and her bright red lips and that white two-piece suit. But the real knockout figure belonged to Maggie Mae, though her navy one-piece suit was conservative, her generous bust fully enclosed, the fabric flaring into a tight swing skirt.

"Just 'cause your help's got the day off," Maggie Mae said, after a sip of the lemonade they were all having, "don't get any ideas. Not only do I *not* do windows, I don't cook on my day off, neither."

Fancy, who was between Maggie Mae and Carmen, laughed and said, "No, *I'll* be fixing supper for you ladies. Chicken with almonds, raisins and white sauce on toast. Curried cabbage on the side, and Lula and I made a chocolate meringue pie this morning."

"You grew up in that house," Maggie Mae said, "I don't figure you ever made yourself more than a glass of water."

Carmen said, "I don't know – those watercress-and-cream-cheese sandwiches in Franny's lunch box are pretty darn good. She shared with me once. You make those yourself, honey?"

"I did," Fancy said.

"Okay," Maggie Mae said, "I'll risk it."

The conversation through the afternoon didn't amount to anything more illuminating than that. The most interesting discussion, between swims, was where to go out tonight.

Lula rattled suggestions off. "How about the Hangover? Or the Knickerbocker Hotel? The Haig on Wilshire? The Jade on Hollywood Boulevard is hep. And the Merry-Go-Round on Vine has this colored boy, Nat King Cole..."

"*Negro man*, girl," Maggie Mae corrected.

"...whatever you wanna call him, he's a wow. Smooth vocals! And he plays the piano like...like..."

"Like *you'd* like to be played," Maggie Mae needled. "You got the nerve, children, we can head to the clubs on Central Avenue, see if you jitterbugs can keep up."

Carmen half-smirked and said, "Most of the places I go you ladies wouldn't like."

"Why?" the others said.

"Most of my crowd is easygoing. But somebody's always spoiling things, giving the Zoot Suiters a bad name. Just too many darn knife fights."

"That'll do it," Maggie Mae said.

"I like the Biltmore," Carmen went on. "Rose and me used to go there before work, sometimes. They got this tea dance in the afternoon and there's lots of unattached Anglo guys around."

"The punctured eardrum patrol," Maggie Mae said.

Fancy asked, "Did Rose know any special guys or...guy...at the Biltmore?"

"Not *a* guy," Carmen said, and sipped lemonade. "Told you before, she was a terrible big flirt."

Maggie Mae said, "Look who's talkin', in that sexy swim suit, midriff all hangin' out."

The younger girl blushed. "Everybody's wearing these! Anyway, there's no men here."

"Not like when Rose wore that halter top to work," Maggie Mae said. "Men was hittin' themselves with hammers."

Fancy said, "You think Rose had something going on in the plant, maybe with Burrows or Dawson?"

Carmen and Maggie Mae shook their heads, but the latter said, "She sure did get cozy with the both of 'em, though. And it's not like there ain't corners and closets around, to go off and find a little privacy."

"The tunnels, for one thing," Carmen said, nodding.

Fancy said, "I didn't know we were allowed down there."

"Well, you're supposed to have a reason to be," Maggie Mae said. "But there's nobody standin' guard or nothin'. Also, during smoke breaks and lunch, that plant empties out. Time enough to hang back and have a little jelly."

Carmen asked, "Like peanut butter and jelly?"

Maggie Mae started laughing. "Girl, I can't decide if you're an ignorant child or one hot mama!"

Everybody laughed but Carmen, who still didn't get it.

Fancy asked, "You girls found Rose, but that teacher, Clara Wallace – was she with you?"

"She hung back with Rose," Maggie Mae said. "Finishing up a section. She was Rose's bucker, y'know."

"I didn't know. You don't mean Clara was there when Rose fell?"

Carmen said, "No, she was in the ladies'. After we found Rose, Clara came up a minute or so later. It hit her hard – they worked together, you know. Left work a few days before she was scheduled to."

Throughout the afternoon and then the meal in the big kitchen, Fancy let up on the questions about Rose. The idea of stepping out tonight fell by the wayside, and Carmen and Maggie Mae gathered their things, made their goodbyes, and walked to the bus stop.

Lula helped clean up. As they did the dishes, Fancy asked, "Do we need to drive over to Studio Hotel to get the rest of your things?"

"That bag I brought? That *is* my things."

"Oh. So...you're all moved in."

"Sure. You want to go outside and carry me over the threshold?"

"Shut up. Listen...how well did you know Rose at the Studio Hotel?"

"Like I said. Not well. Had a few conversations with her. Went out for coffee once and she told me about working in a aircraft plant. Said Amalgamated was a good place to get a job. They were hiring, and unionized and all."

"Did you know about her accident?"

"Don't you mean 'so-called accident'? I did. It got a little play in the papers. I think that had something to do with me deciding to go to Amalgamated, and sort of...take her place."

"Part of the 'V For Victory,' 'Do Your Part' thing."

"Yeah. But would you think less of me if I admitted I hate it there? Not the hard work, but this assembly line crud. Talk about boring! And you get so dirty. I didn't know how good I had it."

Fancy wiped a dish. "What do you mean?"

"Well, I was working at that gas station. Damn, if they didn't give me a cuter uniform than that one you've got! I checked oil, wiped windshields, put gas in, got the money, took the coupon. Easy as pie. Now *this* salt mine!"

"At least you're helping the war effort."

"See, you *do* think less of me."

"But I don't." She touched Lula's shoulder. "You could do better in life than pump gas or rivet. Anyway, these defense jobs will disappear when the guys start coming home."

"Get serious. I didn't even finish high school."

For the first time in her life, Fancy felt guilty for going to Barnard. "Would you mind helping me out tomorrow?"

"Before work? I had a bunch of sleeping planned."

"I want to meet this Clara Wallace."

Lula frowned as she soaped a dish. "What do you need me for?"

"Just to get your take. Your insight. You may not have finished high school, but you've learned plenty I haven't."

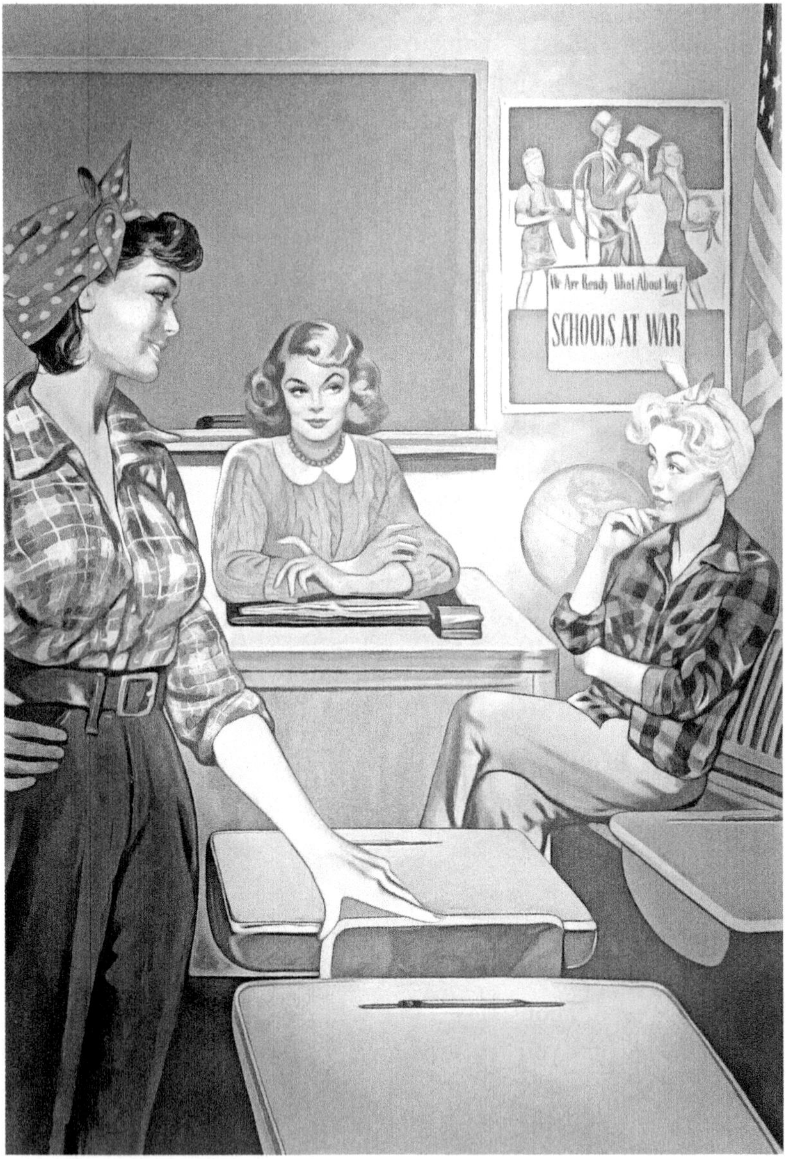
We Are Ready What About You?
SCHOOLS AT WAR

5

BACK TO SCHOOL

"Don't tell me," Lula said, "that you live *here*, too."

Fancy had just pulled in at the curb across and down from a massive white building in the Mission style with ten stairs leading to a trio of archways, a clock tower looming.

"It's our boathouse," Fancy told her deadpan, nodding at the high school on East Chapman Avenue in Fullerton. "Like it?"

Getting from Pasadena to Fullerton had taken forty-five minutes. Fancy had arranged a meeting with Clara Wallace first thing this morning – Lt. Hinder providing a home number – for two p.m. during the teacher's free period.

The drive had been pleasant on the kind of sunny day Southern California residents take for granted. Gas rationing made travel by car much easier in the scant traffic – at least it did when you had a C sticker.

Lula commented, about halfway here, "The way you can just drive around, anywhere you like, is just plain decadent."

"You may not be as familiar with decadence," Fancy replied, "as you think."

Because they would be going straight from Fullerton to Long Beach, the women were in their work clothes. She and Lula both wore plaid shirts and jeans with no cuff, having been informed by a counselor in a skirt that cuffs were a waste of fabric (Fancy had sent her baby-blue coveralls in for repairs). The pair looked almost young enough to be students here, although such casual dress might get them expelled.

Their footsteps echoed down empty hallways and up stairwells as they found their way past lockers that seemed too small, closed doors that murmured with learning, and walls plastered with Homecoming Dance handbills. Life here seemed unchanged, high school a timeless experience, with only the patriotic posters on bulletin boards to hint otherwise.

Fancy knocked at the door to Room 304 and received a crisp, "Come!"

The woman behind the desk was not who Fancy expected Clara Wallace to be – perhaps it was that name, Clara, or the warm alto voice on the phone. This was an attractive woman only a few years older than herself, with reddish brown hair, curly and full, and a wonderful smile with faint freckles trailing across a pert nose – she looked the way Shirley Temple might in just a few years. Her short-sleeve sweater was as pink as Fancy's Packard, her skirt teal, pearls snug at her throat.

Her smile lingering, she rose from the papers she was grading. "I can see you girls are on your way to work. I almost miss it. Almost. Call me Clara."

Fancy and Lula introduced themselves, and immediately the three were on a first-name basis, these veterans of defense plant work. Still, the woman seemed surprisingly young to Fancy, though most of her own high school teachers had been in their twenties and thirties.

Even so, the arm-table school chairs Fancy and Lula slipped into made students out of them, in front of the teacher's desk, where Clara was again seated.

"So you're the two girls," Clara said, her hands folded as she leaned toward them, friendly yet dominant, "who took our places on the line, Rose and me?"

"We are," Fancy said. "As you guessed, Lula and I are on our way to Long Beach now. I just had a few questions and hoped to get some of your thoughts about the accident. The tragedy."

Clara's frown was thoughtful, but also a little suspicious. "I'm still rather fuzzy about what it is you're trying to accomplish, Fancy. Lovely name, by the way. So, you're...a family friend of Douglas Lockhart – is that it?"

Fancy had told the woman a modified version of the truth. She elaborated now, in yet another mix of fact and Fancy.

"I'd already resolved," Fancy said, "to apply at Amalgamated. So I asked Mr. Lockhart, a close friend of my father's, for his advice. He suggested the Long Beach plant and said he'd pave the way."

"Kind of him."

"Yes. But he asked a favor. He had some misgivings about the way the Long Beach police handled the Rose Hannold investigation, and because I've done some work for my father..."

"Head of the Anders detective agency, you said."

"...Yes. Mr. Lockhart asked me, in my spare time at the plant, to look into what happened, unofficially. Just to see what insights I might come away with."

The teacher was smiling again – barely, but smiling. "It's amusing to know that the president of Amalgamated Aircraft thinks there's such a thing as 'spare time' in one of his plants."

"Isn't it?" Fancy said, pleasantly.

Lula looked around her and said, "You seem to be pretty gung-ho on the homefront effort – giving up your summer vacation for war work."

The classroom was heavily decorated with red-white-and-blue posters, a lithograph one depicting marching teenagers ("We Are Ready! Are You?") while homemade examples encouraged buying bonds, planting Victory gardens and mounting salvage drives ("Get in the Scrap!").

"We're asked to emphasize American values and ideals," Clara said. "Of course, as an English teacher, there's only so much of that I can do."

Seemed the propaganda effort went a lot further than just coming up with that Rosie the Riveter campaign.

"And as for our kids," the teacher was saying, "it's very early in the school year, but I see a lot of enthusiasm. We're in the Schools at War program, which encourages students to collect scrap metal, sell war stamps and bonds, and, senior year, enrollees can attend regular classes for four hours if they then work four hours at an Amalgamated plant, helping build planes like I did...and you're doing."

Fancy said, "You obviously take this very seriously."

"I do. My husband flies one of those planes." She frowned again, something different about it this time. "Of course, some people...well, never mind."

"Go on. Please."

She sighed, her fingers intertwined now. "There's another program that, in my opinion, goes a little too far. The Victory Corps...perhaps you've heard of it?"

"No," they both said.

"It puts high school students through training drills, teaches hand-to-hand combat. Over at Roosevelt High, if you were to check out the basement, you'll find girls on their tummies firing rifles at targets down the hall."

Lula said, "May come in handy, later in life, when they run into mashers."

The teacher smiled politely at that, but otherwise let it pass.

"One of the things at Amalgamated that impresses me," Fancy said, "is how well our team works together."

"Oh yes," Clara said, nodding.

"Lula and I rivet and buck."

The teacher half-smiled. "That was my job. *Our* job, Rose and I."

"Did you trade off?" Fancy asked. "Lula and I do. Bucking is so much easier. I don't think I could make it through a day of nothing but riveting."

Clara's smile had something frozen about it now.

Fancy could see the woman was on the verge of saying something, and when Lula seemed about to talk, Fancy held a hand up, just a little, to silence her.

Then the teacher spoke. "I liked Rose. She was *easy* to like. Beautiful, friendly, fun."

Fancy said, "Your co-workers say you took her death hard. That you left Amalgamated a few days before you were scheduled to go."

She shifted in her chair. "Well, the other girls were also working in two-person teams – and Rose and I were rivet-and-bucking, and you can't do that job alone. I guess you two know that as well as anybody."

Fancy asked, "Did Rose rub anybody the wrong way?"

Her head tilted back. "How do you mean?"

"Did she make any enemies on the job?"

"Is that what Mr. Lockhart suspects? Foul play?"

"He just wants a better sense of what happened. He feels, understandably, that a death on the job at his plant sends a bad message to both the employees and the public."

"I *told* you," Clara said, somewhat frostily, "I liked her."

"But," Lula said.

"But...?" the teacher echoed.

"You liked her 'but.' The 'but' was inferred."

"Actually," the teacher said, stiffly, "*implied*."

Lula shrugged. "Sorry. I never finished high school."

Silence fell over the room, as if a final exam was in progress.

Then the teacher said, "Rose could rub me the wrong way. I *did* like her. But you can like people and they can still make you mad. Still irritate. Get on your...wrong side."

"Did she?" Fancy asked. "Get on your wrong side?"

Clara nodded. She looked very young suddenly.

"She was a loafer," the woman said bluntly. "She dogged it. Got away with murder...sorry, sorry. Terrible choice of words."

"And a cliché," Lula said.

They both looked at her.

"I got *that* far in school," Lula said.

Fancy gave her a mildly dirty look.

Clara sighed. Hung her head. "I feel guilty, speaking ill of the dead. But the truth is, she was lazy and she was manipulative. You are both good-looking women. My face doesn't stop clocks, either, frankly. So we all know that we can flirt and tease and handle men if we want to get our way. Want to get out of work. And she did that all the time."

Fancy was sitting forward. "With the lead man – Dawson? And the foreman – Burrows?"

Again Clara nodded; all that curly hair bounced.

"And she *never* riveted," the woman said. "Only bucked. Always took the *easy* job. Well...it's not easy, bucking. But it's not as hard as the other."

"Hold on a second," Lula said, leaning in, like a kid really paying attention in class. "You weren't there when Rose died – you'd gone off to the restroom, right?"

"Correct."

"So Rose would have stepped out from inside the ship's shell onto the platform. I mean, she had to be on that platform to fall off it."

"Yes, that's where she was. She probably got a little stir crazy in there, and when I took that restroom break, she wanted, well...not fresh air, but a change of scenery."

"And fell off the platform?"

"I didn't see it. But presumably, yes, she fell from the platform."

"Stop a moment," Fancy said. "Then tell us what you saw, from the time you came down off that platform until you came back and found that Rose had fallen."

Clara drew a breath, let it out. "As you know, the ladies' room is just down a ways from where we work," she said. "I glanced back and...Rose was on the platform, looking down at the foreman."

"Burrows!" Fancy said. "She was talking to Burrows?"

"Yes. They were just talking. Didn't look like an argument or anything. Couldn't hear anything – there was some noise...a few people always work through the break, very few, but.... Anyway, I walked down to the restroom. Was in there a few minutes."

Fancy said, "And when you returned, the others in the team were already there. With Rose down on the cement."

"No. I was heading back. Saw Joe Dawson crouched over somebody, apparently Rose, his back to me, blocking the view. The platform was empty. I tucked in by one of the B-24s and just watched. He got up and walked off quick."

"See anything in his hands?"

"No." Clara shuddered. "Presumably, he went to call it in...but it was Rose, all right. My heart caught in my throat...I stood there, petrified. The other girls came running up the aisle toward where Rose lay. They didn't see me. Carmen was in the lead, I think." She swallowed. "I just sort of...seized up. Took me a while to get myself back together. A minute or so maybe. Then I joined the girls. I felt...I felt so *guilty*...."

Fancy said, "Why guilty?"

She shook her head. "About the things I'd been thinking about her. Terrible things. Never said a word to her, though. But I did complain to Longtin...."

"The counselor?"

Clara nodded. "And that was stupid. Because I knew Longtin and Rose got along. Rose didn't just cozy up to *men* – she turned the charm on with women, too, if they were in power. I suppose I figured because the Longtin woman was friendly with Rose, and an official with the plant, she'd tell Rose in a nice way to straighten up and fly right. Dumb. Dumb."

She was crying now. From her purse she took a hanky and sobbed into it. Her two guests sat and waited.

Finally Fancy said, "Is there anything else you'd like to share with us?"

Clara shook her head. "That's everything."

"What you told us about Burrows and Dawson at the scene, did you share that with the police?"

"I did. Whether they talked to those two or not, I have no idea."

Lula asked, "Did you tell the other girls about it?"

"No. I'd imagine you know what a gossip mill that plant is. I kept it to myself." She swallowed again. "Ladies, if you don't mind...I have to fix my face before class."

They'd clearly been dismissed.

Fancy thanked the teacher, Lula the same.

But before they were out the door, Clara Wallace called out: "Oh, Miss Hall?"

"Yes?" Lula said.

"There's a new program starting here called Graduate Equivalent Development. Brand new. You can finish high school with some night classes. You strike me as being smart as a whip...if you'll excuse the cliché."

Then, having suggested Lula apply herself, the teacher got out her purse and her compact and started applying herself – her make-up, that is.

On the first smoke break, Fancy headed off to the Administration Building, where she and Lula had gone through the induction process. Head Counselor Sharon Longtin was on the top floor.

Longtin had no secretary, her door standing open on a small, neat office where she was going over documents behind a medium-size desk. As before, the attractive dark-haired, dark-eyed counselor wore a crisp business suit, this one a charcoal gray. She looked up with a smile as Fancy leaned in.

"Miss Longtin," she said, "Franny Allison – I'm over at Building Four."

"Yes, I remember you. You're the one with the witty friend."

"Might be better if I provided my own wit, but yes, Lula's got a mouth on her. Do I need an appointment?"

"My door's always open," Longtin said, and gestured to the visitor's chair opposite her. "Or if it's shut, I'm with someone but won't be long."

Fancy sat. "Don't you also make rounds?"

"I have nine counselors doing that for me. Surely you've seen them."

She had. They were roundly despised, those counselors, walking around in make-up and skirts and never lifting a finger to do anything physical. But the head counselor herself was well-liked – she had desegregated the restrooms, talked Long Beach merchants into extending their hours, and made sure child care was available for all three shifts.

"How can I help you, Franny?"

"I'm trying to fit in with my teammates. Doing all right at it, I guess, but it's clear they really miss that teacher and the poor girl who died. Rose something?"

Longtin nodded gravely. "Hannold. Yes. Tragic. An awful thing. Lovely girl."

"You knew her well?"

The counselor rocked back in her chair. "She was easy to know. Easy to like. Came from a fairly rough background, won a beauty contest, screen test as the prize...but it didn't go anywhere. I thought she'd found a real home here."

"Seems like the only one who didn't get along with her was the other girl who left. That teacher. Sarah."

"Clara. Clara Wallace. Yes, Clara had a few issues with Rose, but nothing serious. Very different backgrounds. Obviously, Mrs. Wallace is college-educated. And she's married. Rose was a little younger and, frankly, I think what she really wanted in life...since her movie dreams were unrealized...was to find a special fella and settle down."

"Do you think Rose knew Clara had problems with her?"

"I doubt it. Frankly, Rose was concerned mostly about Rose. She was young and pretty, and who could blame her?"

"So, then, this teacher complained to you about her?"

"Yes."

"And how did Rose react?"

The counselor stiffened, the dark eyes flaring.

I went too far, Fancy thought.

"I've already said more than I should." Longtin shrugged. "My fault entirely. Rose is gone, so I guess I figured this conversation wouldn't do any harm. But I think that's all I should say. Does this help you better understand the dynamic of the personalities on your team?"

"Yes." Fancy stood. "Yes, it does. Thank you, Miss Longtin. And I'm sorry if I did something wrong..."

A thin smile. "No. I was indiscreet, and that's a sin in my profession. So I'm the one to apologize."

Fancy got up to leave, nodded, but at the door she looked back and said, "Do you think Rose might have *found* that special 'fella,' right here at Amalgamated? Sounds like she was pretty friendly with our foreman and leadman."

The counselor's smile was about as perfunctory as smiles got.

"Good afternoon, Miss Allison. See me again if you have any problems.... Close the door, would you?"

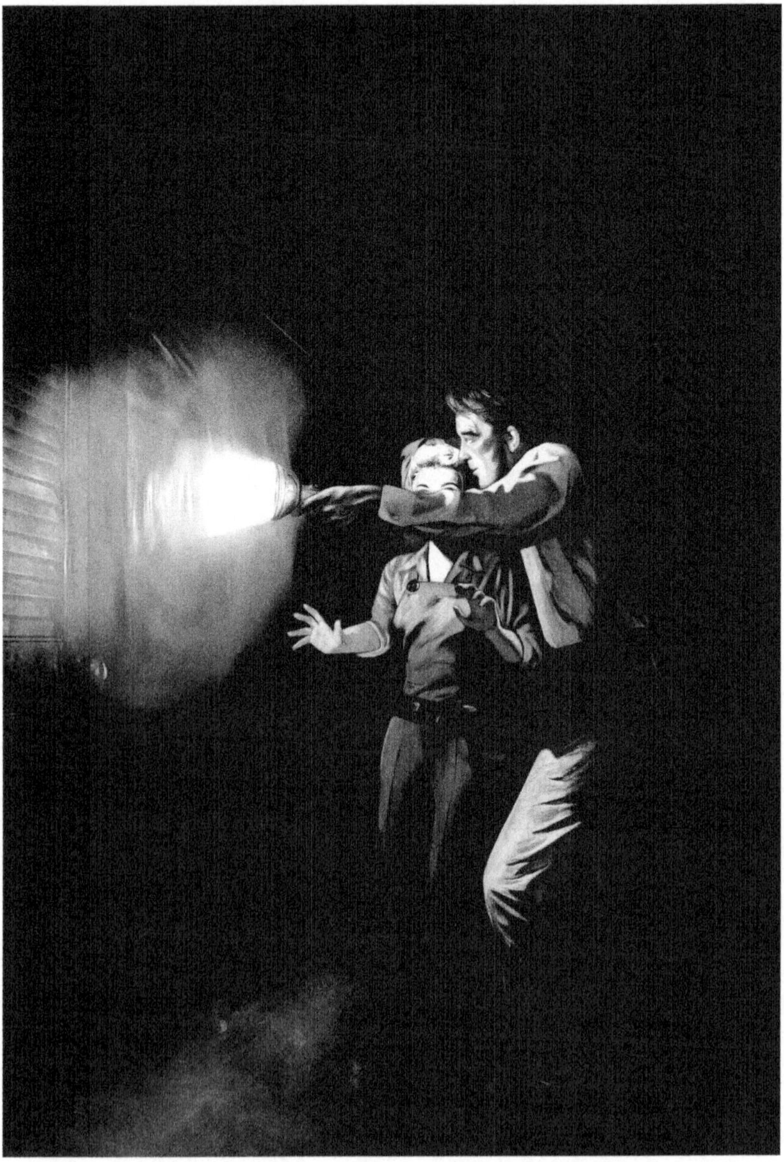

6

TUNNEL OF LOVE

That afternoon, crusty Hank Burrows came around to check the team's progress on the latest B-24 – the powers-that-be were insisting that increased production was a must. One more B-24 per day needed to roll off the line.

"We've got to get things goin', ladies," he told them, rubbing his hands together, as if eager to really dig in next to them. This would have impressed Fancy more if the foreman's hands hadn't been so clean.

As everybody else got back to work, the white-haired old man of maybe forty-five years slipped an arm around Fancy and gave her a smile and a sideways hug. She'd been warned the foreman could get free with his hands.

He smiled and his breath and the yellow of his teeth announced a heavy smoker. "And how are you settlin' in, daughter?"

"Fine, sir."

"I ain't 'sir!' Call me 'Hank,' little lady."

Fancy was almost a head taller than he was.

He removed his arm but stayed close. "Must be hard, fillin' the shoes of that teacher and the poor dead girl."

She saw her opening and took it. "You and Rose got along well, I hear."

"We did at that. Honey of a little gal."

"You must've been one of the last to talk to her."

He blinked. "I was?"

She nodded. "Weren't you talking to Rose shortly before she fell off that platform?"

The foreman backed away. "I never saw a thing!"

"Didn't mean to imply you did." As opposed to infer. "I just heard you were chatting with her right before the accident."

"We chinned now and again, daughter. I like to keep it friendly with you gals."

"I noticed."

He thought about that for a second, then gave her a nod and ambled off, to get familiar with some other female worker, no doubt.

Their leadman, who'd been dealing with the B-24 team next door, came over frowning, which emphasized the squint that made him less good-looking than he thought he was.

Dawson said, "What did *he* want?"

"Production is ramping up."

"Then we gotta get things goin'!"

Foreman and leadmen always said that; it was something they had in common. Like clean hands.

Another similarity – as least with these two – was the way Dawson got too close. She folded her arms and looked at him like a bored babysitter, saying nothing.

"You excited about tomorrow?" the leadman asked. He was a smoker, too.

"What's tomorrow?"

"You'll get word soon enough." He was grinning. "But your lunch break will be a memorable one – may even run long."

"Why?"

"We got a certified movie star comin' to visit. Gonna help give the ol' Gooneybird a push in the papers."

The Gooneybird was the dismissive nickname workers at Amalgamated had come up with for the ungainly C-47 transport. *Did look like it could use a push*, she thought.

"Movie star, huh?" Fancy said. "Who? Errol Flynn? John Garfield?"

"You *wish*, honey. Marla Payne! She'll have the best chassis at Amalgamated tomorrow, including these B-24s and you too, Franny girl."

Dawson strutted off, chuckling.

Payne is right, Fancy thought, troubled by the news. *In the keister....*

Marla Payne was, hands down, Fancy's favorite movie star.

English-born but growing up in Germany from the age of nine, Marla had made a name in silent films and easily moved into talkies in several countries and languages. The cute, petite blonde – starring in dozens of German films throughout the '20s and '30s – was a particular favorite of Hitler's.

But in 1940, with her Jewish heritage a looming threat, she came to Hollywood for a film – she'd already made a handful of others there – and just stayed on, becoming a U.S. citizen in 1941. Since Pearl Harbor, Payne had supported the Allied effort selling bonds and, between Hollywood assignments, doing USO shows.

She had a touch for comedy rivaling Jean Arthur and Margaret Sullivan, which Fancy found irresistible – so different from that other, overly sophisticated émigré, Marlene Dietrich. At one of her mother's charity balls, Fancy had eagerly sought Payne out, making an over-enthusiastic impression; and they had since intersected several other times at various social functions. They had become, if not friends, friendly.

Even in a crowd like this evening's Gooneybird gathering, Payne would recognize her at once. A mere friendly greeting into a microphone could get Fancy's cover blown throughout the entire facility.

She had to do something.

The whistle announced the first smoke break just as one of Building Four's big doors was rising to get ready to roll the Gooneybird out for the ceremony.

Fancy knew where Chip took his break – he always bought a soft drink and popcorn from a little mobile commissary in the plant, and sat along the central aisle, sipping, munching, relaxing by himself. But today she joined him with a bottle of Coke, helping herself to occasional kernels of his popcorn.

He was glad to see her, as they sat there together. "You must be looking forward to this evening," he said. "They're gonna have movie premiere lights and everything."

"Yeah, well that Gooneybird isn't Gable."

"Or Lana Turner, either. But Marla's close. Hey! You *know* her, don't you? I remember you two gabbing at one of your mom's parties."

"That's why I don't wanna go anywhere near there."

"Oh, I get it! You aren't Fancy Anders here. You're...what is it?"

"Franny Allison." Hadn't done any good to get him to say it over and over, had it? He was adorable but thick.

"Yeah," he said, "and you can't have some Hollywood star going around telling your co-workers you're a fraud."

"You're not wrong. Look, I need an excuse not to be around, if the girls or anybody asks. And you're it."

"I am?"

"You are. Is there someplace out of the way we could go and just—"

He was already nodding. "I have just the place. Ever been down in the tunnels?"

"No."

"They're something else. You gotta see for yourself. You know that clerical and stockroom area over there?"

"Where you check out special tools?"

"That's it. There's a locked door between the Gents and Ladies. Meet me at lunch break. Like Jolson says, you ain't seen nothin' yet."

A few minutes before the lunch whistle, Fancy paused in the process of riveting-and-bucking to say to Lula, "I'm skipping the Gooneybird christening. I know Marla Payne a little..."

"Good thing Robert Taylor isn't here," Lula said. "He can't keep his hands off me."

"No, really. I actually do know her, and I don't want my real identity getting around."

"You and Superman. What do I say if any of the other girls ask?"

"Tell them I'm sneaking off with a guy."

"Okay. What will you be doing?"

"Sneaking off with a guy."

On her way to the clerical and stockroom area, Fancy paused at the edge of the big open door for a peek around at the looming Gooneybird, the crowd beyond it already forming in a night crisscrossed by klieg lights. So much for this being a Top Secret location.

She got a glimpse of the petite diminutive little blonde movie star showing her solidarity with the female war workers by wearing a two-piece beige jacket and slacks, smart but vaguely military, her blonde hair in Victory rolls. Marla was chatting with Counselor Longtin, accompanied by Joe Dawson and a handful of other male workers, who were grinning goofily at the celebrity, and lining up for hugs and kisses on the cheek. Several army officers were positioned around and an American flag flapped in the breeze. Soldiers guarded the periphery.

Photographers from all the papers, and probably wire services too, were back here, and Fancy recognized one from the *Times* who would certainly have done the same with her.

Like Marla Payne, Chip Vincent had a military look in his tan

Shantung shirt and slacks – a little nervy, she thought, for a guy ducking the draft by having his daddy get him a job in an aircraft factory. But the blue-eyed blond wasn't hard to look at as she approached him where he loitered near the unlabeled door between restrooms.

"I'll go first," he said. "I know the way."

"I'll bet you do," she said.

He gave her that boyish grin and headed down the narrow, barely lit stairwell. She followed him to a door below, which he went through and so did she.

The passageway was wide enough to easily accommodate a truck, its rounded ceilings home to sporadic conical electric lamps that created pools of light in an unsettling darkness. On either side of the passageway were pairs of double doors every dozen feet or so.

He saw her looking at those and whispered, "Storage. Oil, gasoline, other strategic materials."

"Why are you whispering?" she whispered back.

In his normal voice, which echoed some, he said, "Just seemed like the thing to do. Really, we're not forbidden down here or anything. Plant workers just usually don't have any reason to use these connective tunnels."

She was aware that ramps went down into each tunnel, which she knew were used for the transfer of supplies and materials from one plant to another, often by a small trackless train. And, yes, trucks did drive right down in here. She also knew that upper-echelon types used these tunnels to walk from one building's office area to another.

"Seems awfully deserted," she said.

"That's just because of the Gooneybird hoopla. But somebody might come along." He started down the tunnel, saying over his shoulder, "Come with me."

What choice did she have?

Their footsteps echoed like the sound of a firing squad that didn't have its act together. Chip had brought along a flashlight, though she didn't think he really needed it. Then she realized he was checking the double doors. Above each set of paired knobs was a small slider sign that said, UNAVAILABLE against red. Finally he came to one that said AVAILABLE against green.

He grinned back at her like a naughty little kid and dug a key out of his pocket. He worked it in the lock and opened one of the side-by-side doors and gestured.

"Step into my parlor," he said.

"Leave the door open, Spider."

"Okay, Fly. For now."

It was a big room, even bigger than her kitchen in Pasadena – empty, just a cement chamber, but with a faint suggestion of gasoline in the air.

Well, not entirely empty. There was a thin mattress about the size of what you might find in a jail cell.

"You are a romantic devil," she told him.

"It's not mine exclusively," he said, defensively.

"Much more appetizing now."

He tossed the flashlight on the mattress and it made a *thunk*. He put his hands on her waist and leaned in for a kiss. She put a finger to his lips and shook her head.

"Come on, Fancy. It's not like we never—"

Why, she wondered, *did a man think once you went to bed with him that he had a free pass forever?*

"Chip," she said, "I need more than a grubby mattress and a whiff of gasoline to get romantic. I mean, sweetie – I have a C sticker."

"What are we down here for, then?"

"We're down here because I need to protect my identity."

He nodded. "Like Batman."

"Yeah. Him, too." She touched his face gently. "You're doing me a favor."

"Well, you could do me one."

"No. And if you think you can go caveman on me, think back to that guy I threw through that window at the Mocambo."

He sighed. Nodded. "I brought us a couple of candy bars, in case something like this happened."

"In case something didn't happen, you mean."

"Yeah. I got a Snickers and a Bit-O-Honey."

"I'll take the Snickers. That Bit-O-Honey is the only bit o' honey you're gonna get today."

"Night's not over yet."

"It is for you, sweetie."

They sat on the mattress and had their candy, and that was all.

But she did ask, "How is it you had the key to this storage room?"

"It's a pass key. Fits everything down here."

"And you have it how?"

He shrugged. "Lots of us have 'em. You know guys – whatever it takes to get around the 'no dating on the job' policy.'"

The next day the entire Department 190 team was called to Counselor Longtin's office, and told to skip their first smoke break to do so. Despite the requisite grousing, all the girls were more intrigued than annoyed.

The counselor had moved the visitor's chair aside so that the women – Ethel, Carmen, Maggie Mae, Lula and Fancy (aka Franny) – could stand before her like soldiers reporting to their commanding officer. In such situations you instinctively knew you were either being called on the carpet or about to receive a commendation – no other possibility existed.

"I hope you all enjoyed yesterday's visit from Miss Payne," the counselor said pleasantly.

Everyone nodded and murmured something affirmative.

"We get a lot of support from the Hollywood community," Longtin said. "And it really helps with war bond sales."

Most Amalgamated workers had ten percent of their wages deducted for buying bonds, and events like yesterday's were designed to encourage even more than that.

"And, of course," the counselor was saying, "the publicity value is, in its way, just as important to the war effort as what we do here at the plant. Which is where you ladies come in."

It was?

"What I'm about to ask of you," Longtin said, "is strictly voluntary. But we would like you five women to be on hand for publicity purposes on Monday, first shift – even though that's not your regular work time."

Ethel, in her blunt way, said, "Aren't there any women on first shift worth having their picture took? And nobody never confused me with a pin-up girl."

Longtin almost laughed. "Perhaps not, Mrs. Walsh, but you five women are a perfect cross-section of the women who represent our work force here at Amalgamated – a perfect mix. A hard-working mother of four with a son flying one of our planes. Several pretty young women from assorted backgrounds, including a Mexican-American and a Negro."

Lula, who was obviously liking the sound of this, said, "Don't forget my grandma's a Cherokee. Full-blooded!"

Now Longtin did laugh, a little. "That's good to know. Very good to know."

Ethel, still skeptical, said, "What does this deal consist of?"

"Just getting your pictures taken doing your job."

"Do we need to spruce up?"

"A little sprucing up wouldn't hurt. The important thing is that you're willing to participate, and to come in a full shift before your regular one starts. And Monday is the day you're needed."

"Why Monday?" Fancy asked.

Longtin paused. She was clearly thinking about whether to say more. Finally she did.

"It's very hush-hush, but an important dignitary will be making an appearance at the plant. Yesterday, with Miss Payne, was something of a dry run. On this next occasion, there'll be even more security."

The women exchanged raised-eyebrow glances.

"Now," Longtin said, "you're not to say a word, and of course you've all signed the Espionage Act, so when I say you need to keep this to yourselves, you understand."

The women all nodded, and one by one said yes to participating, though Ethel was the last to chime in.

"You seem reticent, Mrs. Walsh," Longtin said.

"What does that mean?"

"Reluctant."

"Well, it's just...I never had my picture took."

Everyone smiled and Longtin assured Ethel it would be painless. Fancy lingered after the others left.

"Miss Longtin," she said, "I need to get permission from my parents before posing for any publicity pictures. They were against my taking a job here, and are frankly rather rabidly anti-FDR and—"

"How on earth," Longtin said sharply, "did you know the dignitary I mentioned is the President?"

She hadn't! She'd merely been looking for an excuse to get out of it, at least until getting a chance to talk to Uncle Doug and Rick Hinder and see if she could continue her investigation under her real name, which would certainly have been exposed.

"Just a hunch," Fancy said. "I didn't figure you'd make such a fuss for anything, or anybody, less important."

Longtin mulled that for a moment, then said, "Well, think it over. You're not crucial to this effort. After all, we have three lovely girls without you. And Ethel."

Fancy nodded and started out slowly.

"But you *are* the prettiest girl in the plant," Longtin said with a teasing smile.

Of course, Fancy already knew that.

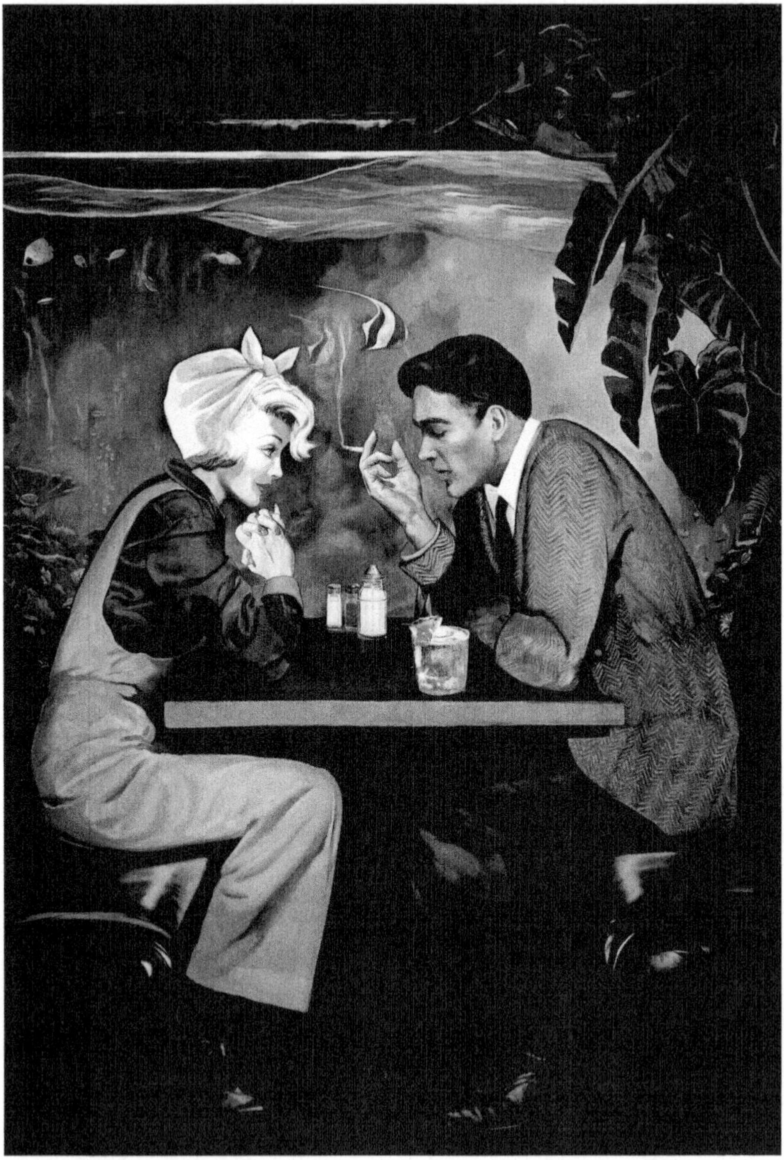

7

DOWN THE PIKE

B y day, the unlighted vertical neon sign saying

      D
      A
      M
      O
      N'
      S

was as dull as the gray facade promising COCKTAILS and THICK STEAKS. But Fancy knew, from past experience, that an exotic – if imaginary – land awaited within. The South Central Avenue Polynesian-themed restaurant in Glendale was fifteen minutes or so from Fancy's Pasadena homestead. She'd left Lula behind to fend for herself in the kitchen's shockingly well-stocked wartime fridge and would swing by to pick her up for work after the two p.m. lunch meeting with Lt. Rick Hinder.

Fancy had been calling the police detective every day or so to report in, and now needed him to help her come to a decision.

A few couples were at tables and booths, lingering after lunch, as she trekked under a thatched ceiling past plastic palm trees and rattan-covered walls with murals of Polynesia by artists who'd never been there but were familiar with Dorothy Lamour movies. Carved masks mingled with stuffed toy monkeys as she made her way through a friendly forest of palm fronds, fishnets, spears, Tiki gods and fake orchids, pausing at the sizable aquarium of tropical fish. An outrigger canoe hanging from the ceiling pointed to a bar in back.

A few regulars were chatting with an Aloha-shirt-sporting bartender as jukebox music loaded up with nothing but island records, apparently, added ambience, thankfully at a low decibel level – "Pagan Love Song" at the moment. Rick was waiting in a booth, working on a Mai Tai – he was not the sort of cop who stood on ceremony where a no-drinking-on-the-job policy was concerned.

The detective's gray herringbone jacket looked sharp, off-the-rack or not, and his charcoal tie went well with his dark hair and eyes. He gave her a smile that made the lucky bum look even more like Tyrone Power than he already did. He half rose within the booth.

"You look cute in that," he said, nodding at her, as she slid in across from him.

"I have to head to work after," she said, referring to the baby-blue coveralls, their grease stains gone (for now) and the knee neatly sewn. Her blouse was a darker blue and she wore her usual white work turban.

Also very light make-up. She didn't need this would-be lover-boy getting any ideas.

He was smoking, a confirmed Chesterfields man. But he'd put his latest one out as she approached – a nice gentlemanly gesture, she had to admit.

"Before we get started," he said, in his mellow second tenor, folding his hands, "there's something personal I need to share."

She almost asked him not to, but something stopped her.

"Lois has filed for divorce," he said. "I'm not going to contest it. It's been a long time coming."

"I'm sorry."

He shrugged. "I get the kids, summers, and one weekend a month, rest of the year. Grounds are cruel treatment, but I wanted you to know I didn't do anything with Lois to deserve that."

Except run around on her.

"I mean, I'm no saint," he said, reading her. "No angel. But you gotta have grounds, right?"

She said nothing.

"I just thought you might like to know."

"That you're no angel?"

He shrugged. "Just...what my status was. Is."

"We should get to business. I'm on a schedule."

Suddenly he seemed a little nervous, or maybe he already had been. "Sure. Like one of these Mai Tais?"

"No thanks. Alcohol and riveting don't mix."

"...Here's the waitress."

They ordered – a shrimp cocktail for her, a steak sandwich for him.

As the girl went off, Rick grinned and said, "Gotta love these un-rationed restaurants. Of course, half the time they're out of what you want. So. What do you have for me?"

Fancy told him about the P.R. photo session she'd been asked to be part of, but she did not mention the visit from FDR. Rick might be her police contact, but she was still hampered by the Espionage Act...even if she *had* signed a false name.

"I'm afraid I've called attention to myself," she said, "trying to get out of something most girls would kill for. That counselor may already be suspicious."

"I wouldn't worry," Rick said, waving it off. "But, yeah, I can see the spot you're in. You've been in the papers too often under your real name to risk turning up under a fake one."

She nodded, saying, "And there's a good chance a *Times* photographer will be there," and told him how she'd managed to duck out of the Marla Payne event.

"I'm starting to think," she said, "that going undercover at the plant was a dumb idea in the first place."

"Fancy, I can't agree. I always thought it was a natural."

She half-smirked. "You'd *think* it would be. But I spend all my time on the job...except for smoke breaks and 'lunch' with my co-workers. And I haven't even got much out of that."

An instrumental version of "Blue Hawaii" was playing over speakers.

"The teacher who quit gave you some nice tidbits," Rick said. "Like, I hadn't heard that foreman, Burrows, was seen hanging around Rose just minutes before her death. And I didn't know Dawson was first on the scene – I thought Carmen Cervantes and your other co-workers found Rose's body."

"The Long Beach detectives hadn't informed you? Or maybe they didn't know any of this."

He shook his head. "I followed up with them, after you told me about your visit with Clara Wallace. They knew, all right – they just didn't think either item was important enough to note in their reports. They talked to Burrows, who said he didn't see anything, and what's suspicious about a foreman talking to one of his people? As for Dawson rushing away from the body, he says that was to call the accident in."

"If it *was* an accident."

"If it was an accident." Rick leaned forward. "Look, Fancy – maybe you *can* keep investigating, in a casual way, even after your real name comes to light. You're enough of a celebrity that using a false name at the plant wouldn't be unusual – particularly if the president of the company, your old family friend, knew you were doing it."

"Come on, Rick – what am I accomplishing there besides getting dirty, sweaty and sore as hell for days on end?"

"Helping the war effort?"

"I think you should either officially re-open this investigation...or move on. So *I* can move on."

"Why, are you convinced Rose *wasn't* murdered?"

She sighed. "I wish I had an opinion. Oh, there are possible murder suspects, certainly – men she flirted with, women she annoyed. But their motives are thin. I mean, Rose Hannold was a tease – that's pretty clear. But can you see a guy killing a girl just because she won't put out?"

His smile turned a little wicked. "You're asking me?"

She almost smiled. "Come on. These just aren't credible murder motives. Kill a girl 'cause she's lazy? Or for leading some guy on? I don't buy either one."

"Maybe there's a motive we haven't thought of yet."

"It's a dangerous workplace," she told him. "There are plenty of ways to get maimed or killed in a plant like that, without any help. Rose may have just...taken a bad fall."

"A really bad fall.... Here's our food."

They ate in silence, lost in thought as Bing Crosby crooned "Sweet Leilani," followed by Tommy Dorsey's "Hawaiian War Chant," and a few others.

When it was time to go, Rick left a five and walked Fancy out.

On the sidewalk, he said, "Let me talk to ol' Uncle Doug about this. Get his opinion. Find out if he wants this thing dropped...or maybe have you skip the photo shoot and keep poking around. *Or* pose for the cameras *and* go on investigating, under your own name. *Something.*"

"I'm fine with whatever he wants me to do," she said, shaking her head. "Or not do."

He was studying her, sunshine making him squint. "It's not like you, Fancy."

"What isn't?"

"Being so unsure of yourself."

She frowned at him. "Rick. The truth. Do you think I'm in over my head?"

"I don't know. I really don't. But if there's some motive we've missed, a murderer who may be using the dangers in that war plant to cover his or her tracks...you better be ready to bail out on a dime, baby. I don't want you dying on me. Not when I'm a single man again."

He kissed her on the forehead and was gone before she could object.

Or approve.

―――

Sunday evening found Fancy and Lula in the pink Packard, dressed to the nines, doing something the duo never imagined they would – head back down to Long Beach on their day off.

A War Worker Salute at the Majestic Ballroom was drawing them – and many other girls and women from Amalgamated – to that sleazy but exciting waterfront area known as the Pike. Admission was free for women with war jobs! Everybody was going.

Well, not everybody. Wife and mother Ethel opted out, and the only Negroes welcome at the Pike's amusement park were those hired to taunt white patrons into playing the disgusting "Dunk the Darkie" game. Fancy was glad Maggie Mae had a big night planned in L.A. at the Orpheum Theater, where white and Negro entertainers and a mixed audience got along just fine.

The amusement park sprawled at the end of the Red Car electric line from Los Angeles along the shoreline south of Ocean Boulevard, females from defense plants all over the area pouring in, decked out in their smartest dresses. Fancy and Lula met Carmen at the park's archway entrance, then strolled down the glittering Walk of a Thousand Lights past arcades, food stands, gift shops, shooting galleries, tattoo parlors, palm readers, spook houses, sideshows, and Dodge 'Em Cars (for those frustrated by gas rationing).

The neon-festooned midway – the din of pinball machines and carny barkers and crowd laughter rivaling Amalgamated's mechan-ical uproar – thronged with war workers, sailors on liberty, furloughed troops, and pretty young females who were the greatest attraction of all.

Between the Strand Theater and across from the Cyclone roller coaster, which took screaming riders out over the waves, the three women spotted the neon announcing the

Majestic
BALL ROOM

where jitterbugging was frowned upon, and couples were forbidden by city ordinance from dancing cheek to cheek. Fancy felt confident neither rule would apply tonight.

Inside they found a world of cream-colored walls, oval lacquer tables, drifting cigarette smoke, red-white-and-blue bunting, and good-looking young people, dancing to the music of Neal Gianni's Swing Band, "popular on radio and record," though Fancy had never heard of them. The gleaming dance floor was immense – the Majestic was a former skating rink, Lula said – with a draped fabric ceiling hanging in faux light-blue waves. Fittingly, the Swing Band was doing a pretty fair job with the Dorsey version of "Blue Skies."

The ballroom served no liquor, but Fancy and Lula got soft drinks at the stands on either side of the vast room, and flasks from pockets and purses were being passed around like this was 1922, not '42. Females wore bright floral and dotted prints with shoulders either bared or padded, skirts long and sleek, though the jitterbug girls wore knee-length skirts and bobby sox. Males preened in sport coats and ties, both Windsor and bow, or sometimes Cuban-collared sport shirts.

She and Lula were getting plenty of looks from sailors and GIs – Fancy in a rose dress with lacy bib collar, hair in Victory rolls worthy of Marla Payne; Lula in a navy dress with white chevron stripes on skirt, cuffs and sleeves.

In Fancy's opinion, however, Carmen won the night with her Zoot look – gray fingertip coat with black sleeves, lipstick so red it was almost black, big earrings, knees showing. And that high black pompadour! Other *Pachucha*-style girls were scattered about, and the Mexican boys in their own wild Zoot suits zeroed in on them.

The Zoot Suiters sometimes got a dirty look from the "anglos" (as Carmen called them), but to Fancy, particularly when couples danced to upbeat numbers like "Boogie Woogie Bugle Boy," she thought they looked great. Carmen was out there doing that right now.

"They're stunned," Lula said.

"Who is?"

"These sailor boys and dogfaces. Intimidated. They think you're Lana Turner and I'm Hedy Lamarr."

"It's an honest mistake."

"If it was Sadie Hawkins Day, and Gary Cooper and Charles Boyer were here, I wouldn't be afraid to ask 'em to dance. These Hollywood stars take their pants off one leg at a time like anybody else."

"I think that's put their pants *on* one leg at a time."

"You say tomato, I say to-mah-to."

A sailor was coming over, grinning like Alfalfa in the Our Gang comedies.

"Don't look now, Hedy," Fancy said, "but I think you're about to be drafted."

"Yikes. Or shanghaied."

While Lula danced with the sailor to "I'll Remember April," Fancy studied the crowd. Something had already struck her as odd....

Many familiar faces from the plant, male and female, were here enjoying themselves, although the nature of the work meant she knew only her own teammates well. But one person stood out – their leadman, Joe Dawson.

He looked handsome enough tonight, a rare man in a suit – a Victory suit, she could tell, rayon replacing restricted natural fiber, short jacket, narrow pants, single-breasted coat. His red-and-yellow striped tie, though, was on the loud side.

That made Dawson conspicuous in a crowd dominated by uniformed military and casually dressed young guys; but that was not what caught her attention. It was how he worked the room, going around and talking to various women, always unaccompanied ones, getting very chummy, lots of smiles. Like he was really putting on the make.

But it never went anywhere. None ever accompanied him to the dance floor. He bought no drinks. They just talked. And always the woman sat alone at the moment – if she were here with any other females, they were out on the floor with a sailor or soldier or civilian.

When Lula came back, saying, "Now *that* was a war effort," Fancy said, "Something odd about our loveable leadman over there."

She told Lula what she'd seen and asked her opinion.

"Well, I think he's a jerk, but I could be wrong. He might be a drip. Or maybe a dope. I'm gonna say a dope."

"He's not a dope," Fancy said. "He doesn't exactly have brains, but there's something shrewd about him."

Lula was glancing over at Dawson as he talked to yet another female. They all seemed to Fancy a little on the hard side; but then these were hard days, and nights.

"Are you really surprised," Lula asked, "that Dawson's striking out, again and again? Do *you* want to date that wolf?"

"Not hardly," Fancy said with a shiver.

"Hi, girls," someone said. Someone male.

The band began to play "You Made Me Love You."

Chip Vincent said, "Dance with me, Fance? For old times' sake?"

The boyish blond looked collegiate in a sport shirt and gray-and-black glen plaid sport coat with leather elbow patches. He seemed embarrassed, whether for his behavior the other day or just in general, she couldn't say.

What she did say was "Sure," and got up and accompanied him to the dance floor.

"Cheek to cheek's against the rules," she reminded him.

"Against the law, actually. Anyway, I wouldn't think of it."

That hurt her, mildly. "Oh?"

"Not that I wouldn't enjoy it."

They glided along together. He danced well. And, of course, so did she.

"Look," he said, "about that, uh, tunnel incident..."

So it was an "incident" now.

"Yes?" she said innocently.

"Sorry if I was out of line."

"Out of line escorting me into a gas-reeking room with a jailhouse mattress on the floor?"

"I didn't get really fresh or anything. You have to admit that."

"Oh, yes, you were a real gentleman."

"You could at least thank me for the Snickers."

She laughed. "You've given me plenty of snickers, Chip, in our time together. Say, uh...do you know who Joe Dawson is?"

"He's your leadman, isn't he?"

"Yes. He's here tonight. It's just...something odd. He's chatting up one woman after another and not getting anywhere."

"Tell me about it."

"It just seems...off-kilter, somehow."

He glanced toward Dawson. "Well...don't quote me on this, but there's a rumor going around."

"Yes?"

"You know there used to be, uh, houses of ill repute around here, near the Pike? But they all got shut down when the navy and army bases geared up. Anyway, word is Dawson is on his *own* recruiting drive lately – to get girls to sleep with soldiers and sailors. Piecework you might say.... Song's over, Fance. Another dance?"

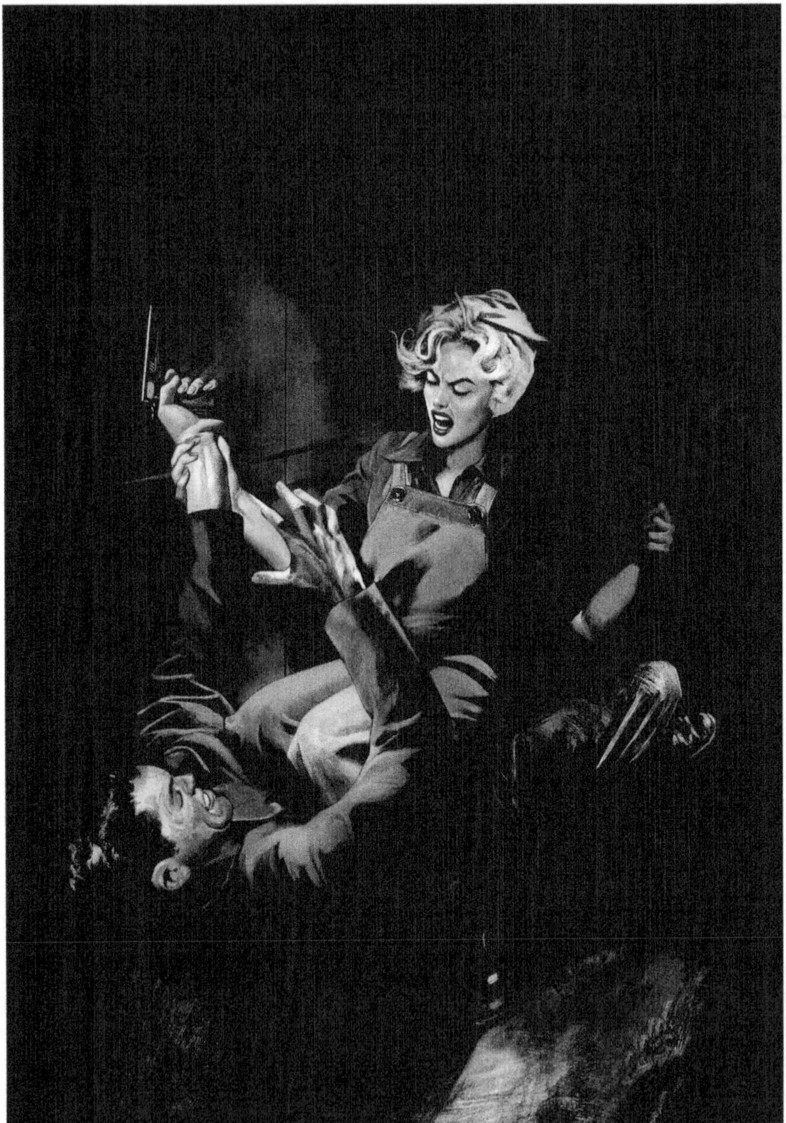

8

RETURN TRIP

Monday morning, at eight a.m., Fancy, Lula and the rest of the team were at Counselor Sharon Longtin's office, lined up for inspection in front of her desk.

The seated counselor looked each woman over.

Fancy wore her trademark baby-blue coveralls with a new red-and-white striped top, properly patriotic, and her familiar white turban; her tool belt was slung around her waist like a western marshal's bullet-studded holster.

Lula, for the first time, wore the cute gas station jumpsuit she'd once mentioned to Fancy, her brunette hair tucked under a snug cap with a bill.

Not surprisingly, Carmen wore a fingertip coat and baggy slacks, her pompadour protected by a white cotton hairnet. Maggie Mae was in blue-denim coveralls that looked brand-new as did the red-and-black bandanna over her hair.

Ethel was the surprise. She, too, had apparently bought herself something for the occasion – tan coveralls with a dark brown work cap and, most shockingly, the gaunt beauty of her features had been brought out by lightly, even expertly, applied make-up.

"You girls really look lovely," Longtin said with a smile. "Ethel, you're a revelation."

Ethel harumphed. "You don't think I got four kids by bein' no hag, did you?"

Gentle laughter applauded that, though Ethel for the life of her didn't seem to know why.

"Ladies," Longtin said, hands folded, all business, "your shift has been swapped with first – that is to say, they will be coming in for you tonight."

Confused and maybe a touch irritated, Lula said, "So we're gonna work this morning, then?"

Longtin waved that off. "No, you're not working at all. You don't have to worry about getting your spiffy clothes mussed. The only thing on your agenda is the photo shoot. Now, initially you'll be meeting and posing with our distinguished visitor, who arrives here in two hours."

Maggie Mae asked, "Is who he is a secret till he shows? Or is he a 'her' – Eleanor Roosevelt maybe?"

Longtin smiled again. "You are *warm*, Miss King. It's her husband."

"The President!" Maggie Mae blurted.

"The President," Longtin said, with an affirming nod.

Only Fancy showed no reaction, since this was hardly news to her; but the rest were agape with excitement.

"The President will be at Amalgamated for only an hour," the counselor was saying, "and just a small part of that with you. The photo session proper will take place while he's touring the rest of the plant. An OWI photographer will be taking your official pictures, but representatives of the local and national press will be shadowing Mr. Roosevelt while he's here."

The women looked at each other, mouths moving but nothing coming out. This was the most exciting thing that had happened to any one of them, with the exception of Fancy, of course, who had met several presidents and a king or two.

"Now, please go to the cafeteria and relax," the counselor said. "We'll come and collect you when it's time. But, uh...let's not overdo the coffee. We don't want to interrupt a Presidential meeting with bathroom breaks or caffeine-induced hysteria."

Everyone laughed, again except for Fancy, who had other things on her mind.

"I'll be a minute," Fancy told her co-workers as they went out, and when they had, she closed the door and said to Longtin, "May I?" She gestured to the visitor's chair that had been set aside to make room for the inspection.

"We have to quit meeting like this," Longtin said, mildly amused, but she nodded to the chair and Fancy dragged it over and sat, collecting her thoughts.

Fancy had called Rick Hinder first thing this morning, to see what her Uncle Doug wanted her to do about this awkward situation.

But Rick had said, "I haven't been able to get through to him. He's in Washington, D.C., taking secret meetings, incommunicado. I'm trying."

"Well, this visiting dignitary, and an army of photogs, will be here before you know it. What should I do?"

"I'll stay in my office until I get through to the man. Check in with me by phone every now and then, if you're able."

She had done that once already and Rick hadn't had any better luck than before.

Now she was seated across from Sharon Longtin, who looked so very Joan Crawford professional in her suit and perfectly coiffed hair, a long black bob curling under. "How can I help you, Miss Allison?"

She leaned forward. "That's the thing, Miss Longtin. It's not 'Miss Allison' – it's Miss Anders. Francine Anders."

The counselor leaned back. She frowned, not in anger or even irritation – more like trying to bring the creature seated before her into focus.

"Fancy Anders," Longtin said, thinking aloud. "The socialite. I've seen you in the papers! Ball gowns and motorcycles and fashion shows and boat races...."

"Yachts actually. Well, schooners. Listen, that's why I shouldn't be posing for any photos, at least not as Franny Allison."

Quickly but completely, she filled the woman in, including Rose's starring role in the Rosie the Riveter campaign, and her own undercover investigation.

"What happened to Rose Hannold was classified an accident," Longtin said, looking mildly flummoxed. "There was an inquest...."

"Yes, but Uncle Doug...Mr. Lockhart...doesn't believe her death was accidental."

She told the counselor of the phone call the Amalgamated president had received from Rose the night before she fell.

All business again, Longtin asked, "Miss Anders, do you have any reason to think that Rose may have been murdered?"

"I *have* encountered people who were unhappy with her – a co-worker who thought she was lazy, others who saw her come on to men...men who thought she was easy when she was really just a flirt. Nothing worth killing anybody over."

"This publicity push you mentioned...Rose the Riveter?"

"Rosie, actually."

"Could the girl have been killed to derail that? It wouldn't be the first time a defense plant's been targeted for sabotage."

"I don't think so. The OWI would just cast someone else in the part of hard-working female war worker. Maybe this visit from FDR this morning is part of that."

Longtin sighed. "Maybe it is. I admit I'm feeling a bit...left out. I should have been told about this Rosie the Riveter campaign. It would have alerted me to Rose's death as possibly more than just an industrial accident. And I wish I'd been told who you really are, and what you were up to here, as an undercover operative. We could have worked in tandem."

"We can start right now," Fancy said. "I can tell the girls who I am – can't have them caught flatfooted in this thing – and the photo shoot can go on with me as a society girl who picked up a riveting gun for the cause."

"That works for me," Longtin said, nodding. "Have you checked with Mr. Lockhart about this?"

"I've tried. My police contact is trying to get in touch with him even now. But Uncle Doug is behind closed doors in D.C., in meetings that have to do with things well above my pay grade."

"And mine, obviously," Longtin said. "Let's go ahead with it, then. Maybe *you'll* be the new Rosie the Riveter."

Fancy stood. "I'm not sure that's a good idea. With my history, I'm not the all-American girl the government would probably prefer."

"Who is?" Longtin said, rising behind her desk. She extended a hand. "Thank you, Fancy. I think this is going to work out."

The women shook hands.

Fancy paused at the door and said, "Oh, one other thing. Are you aware of the rumor about girls here at the plant being recruited for prostitution?"

Obviously alarmed, Longtin said, "No! Nothing like that."

Fancy wandered back a few steps and told the counselor what she'd observed at the Majestic Ballroom – Joe Dawson chatting up one girl after another but never escorting her to the dance floor much less taking her by the arm and out the door.

"Dawson's a good leadman," Longtin said. "It's hard to believe he'd be part of anything like that."

"He's pretty familiar with the girls under him...so to speak. I'll keep an eye on him."

"I'll do some discreet asking around about him," she said, then let out a breath. "I'll see you in the cafeteria around a quarter till ten.

To collect your teammates for the Presidential visit and the photo shoot."

"Right," Fancy said. "Just another typical day at Amalgamated."

In the Administration Building lobby, Fancy slipped into one of a row of telephone booths and checked in with Rick Hinder again.

"Nothing yet," he said. "I was able to find out that Lockhart's staying at the Mayflower in D.C., and that's a start. I'll stay on it."

"Maybe you don't need to," she said. "I've decided to go through with the photo shoot, and to stay on a while and keep investigating, in between riveting and bucking. I filled Counselor Longtin in and she encouraged it."

"Your Uncle Doug may see it otherwise."

"He can pull me off the line and out of here if he likes. But until he does, I'm staying. I finally have a lead, after all."

"What lead is that?"

She suddenly realized she hadn't mentioned the rumor about prostitution. She reported it.

"I'll talk to my counterpart on the Vice Squad," Rick said, "and see if it resonates. But I don't really see how it could tie in with Rose Hannold. Didn't you say she was a tease?"

"Yes, and probably a virgin, by all accounts."

"Not a good prospect for a call girl."

"Not really, no."

"Listen, try to check in with me before that photo session. Do you have any idea who this big mucky-mucky visitor is?"

"Not a clue," she lied.

Soon she found herself walking the same route she'd taken that first day and on so many since. Only this morning was different. Yes, she was under the same sky obscured by camouflage netting that separated her from it, and there was that now-familiar outdoor stage with its "Work to Win" banner, and the bus stop and tool store and infirmary....

But this time soldiers were everywhere, positioned here,

patrolling there, as if the plant had been invaded by the country's own military. And she supposed it had – what more precious American asset was there to guard than Franklin Delano Roosevelt?

In addition to the tan khaki uniforms, however, were the dark suits, bland neckties and dark sunglasses of anonymous-looking men who seemed to roam at will. When she entered the plant, putting her goggles on and earplugs in, she saw more of this dark-suited breed – some seemed to be stationed at posts, others prowled, moving slow but steady down the central aisle, weaving in and out and around ongoing work. Fancy figured these invaders were either FBI or Secret Service or both.

She paused at Department 190, their latest B-24 unattended in the midst of the usual bustle of activity all around – no one on a ladder, platforms empty though the one under the bomb bay had the usual collection of motors, lights and stools left conscientiously by the night shift who'd followed Fancy's team in on Saturday night.

"Allison!"

She turned and a figure in a khaki jumpsuit was trotting up the central aisle toward her – Joe Dawson.

Meeting him halfway, she asked, "What is it?"

"You on your way to the cafeteria to meet up with your girlfriends?"

"I was heading there, yes. Why?"

He gestured vaguely. "Supposed to help you pick up some nice new shiny tools over at the stockroom. I guess they want you ladies lookin' your best for the cameras."

She shrugged. "Okay."

"I'll give you a hand."

"Not necessary."

"Not what I heard. It's a couple of heavy toolboxes."

She shrugged, and they turned back the way he'd come and walked through the controlled chaos of the busy, noisy plant, sparks flying, metal clanging.

He grinned at her. That handsome face wasn't quite undone by the squinty eyes. "You didn't say hello at the Majestic last night."

"Neither did you. You seemed occupied."

They walked a while. The screech of a circular saw shearing through metal sounded like a jungle bird fighting for its life.

He said, good-naturedly, "Nobody was buyin' what I was sellin'."

"What were you selling, Joe?"

He grinned. "Just my natural charm, kid. My ever-lovin' natural charm."

She didn't take it any further. Lots of crazy rumors like Chip's flew around a place like this; for all she knew, Dawson had just been trying to get lucky at the Majestic and hadn't gotten anywhere.

She recalled a guy she'd gone out with in college, a star quarterback, who had come up to her at a dance and said, "You wouldn't want to go to bed with me, would you, beautiful?" The next morning she had said to this handsome louse, "Does that line work for you often?"

"About once in ten tries," he said. "You were the first 'yes' after six 'no's last night."

Maybe that was the real story of Joe Dawson.

The clerical and stockroom area was just ahead. She glanced to her right, where the leadman had been in step with her, and realized he'd fallen in behind her.

Right behind her.

Something poked her in the small of the back. Something hard. Metallic hard.

"That's my little Baby Browning," he whispered in her ear, just loud enough to make it through her earplug. "Don't wake her up or she'll spit a .25 slug. Take a right."

They were adjacent to the restroom area and she knew what he had in mind – that door between the Gents and Ladies, the portal to the tunnel below....

The hell of it was people were all around, at least to their left they were – women and a few men caught up in the usual hurry and scurry of work. First half of shift was always like this. Took a meal break to slow the metabolism down. Nobody was watching. And if they had been, what would they have seen? A leadman following a worker close behind? So what?

She was at the unlabeled door.

"Open it," he said.

She did.

"Go on," he told her.

And she did, stepping in, with him right behind her, shutting them into near darkness.

Paused at the top landing, she said, "You're out of your mind. There are feds and soldiers all over the place. They'll be patrolling these tunnels."

"No, the tunnels are sealed off. And the doors to entrances like this are all locked."

"We just went through one!"

"Which I unlocked before I collected you, honey. I have a passkey. Now go. Go on down."

She went.

Then, reaching the bottom, she paused again.

He stuck the snout of the little automatic in her neck. The metal was cold. The coldest thing she ever felt, except maybe the sound of his voice.

"I said go," he snarled. With all his natural charm.

She opened the door and stepped into the tunnel, and he followed, their footfalls echoing as did the door as he closed it, though he hadn't slammed it. The passage seemed even bigger than on her previous visit, the pools of light punctuating the blackness lending an eerie unreality. All that clamorous activity above and nothing here but silence broken only by her breathing and her host's, and their footsteps, as he prodded her down the passage at right.

Chip had used a flashlight to find just the right double doors among many, but Dawson didn't need one. That was both disturbing and made all this darkness occasionally relieved by pools of light feel all the more consuming.

She said, her voice resonating off the rounded ceiling, "So is that what this is about? You're just a cheap pimp?"

"Shut up."

"I'll be missed, and those feds will come looking."

"Good luck to them."

"They'll come to you. Longtin knows I suspect you. So does Lula Hall."

"Does she? Good to know."

They kept going, but then a hand grabbed onto her shoulder and brought her to a stop.

He reached past her and opened a side-by-side door, not using a key. He'd unlocked this one in advance, too. He planned ahead, their leadman. Well, he'd always been fairly well-organized....

"Get in," he said, behind her again.

The darkness awaiting was penetrated by just enough light for her to make out barrel upon stacked barrel of what had to be gasoline, by the smell of it.

She dropped to her knees and grabbed behind her, gripping his ankles and yanking, jerking, taking him down on his back, hard. She flipped on top of him and both her hands went to the wrist holding the little automatic.

But he was a big man, and a strong man, and when his left fist slammed into her side, all the wind rushed out of her and her grip on his wrist turned into a bunch of loose fingers. She had the barest sense of his hand with the Baby Browning in it, whipping toward her, and the flat barrel catching her in the side of her head.

Then darkness, unrelieved even by conical pools of light.

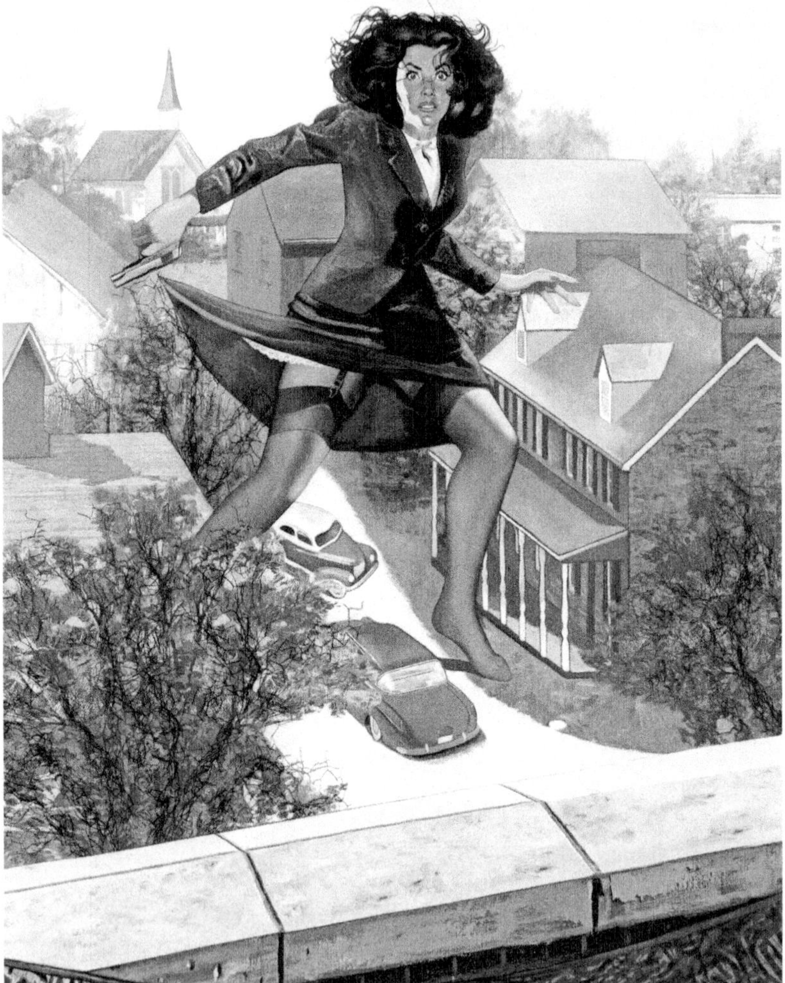

9

TOOLS OF THE TRADE

Fancy awoke to pitch black.

Finding herself sprawled on a cement floor, she sat up and waited for her head to stop spinning. How long she'd been out, she had no idea. She touched the side of her head where she'd taken the blow – her turban had absorbed some of it, and was now sticky with blood. That viscous dampness on the cloth indicated she hadn't been out long enough for the blood to fully dry.

She removed the turban and tested the wound. More stickiness, but any bleeding had stopped; some swelling but no gash. Somewhat unsteadily, she got to her feet and regained her bearings. The slightest edge of light ran along the bottom of side-by-side doors.

What had happened to her was clear.

Dawson had struck her, knocking her out, and shoved her inside the storage chamber. She was just inside the double doors now. Her hands confirmed as much, including, predictably, that he'd locked her in.

The stench of gasoline further confirmed that this was almost certainly the storage chamber she'd caught a glimpse of before Dawson clubbed her – a big room, yes, even bigger than her kitchen in Pasadena, stacked with drums of fuel. The chamber was packed with the containers – the area remaining (in which she found herself) shallow. She only had to turn and walk a few steps before she felt their ribbed rounded surfaces.

Her head had cleared by now, though she was sickened by the smell of the gas, which initiated a headache and nausea. A loud ticking penetrated her protective earplugs; for a few moments she thought what she heard was her watch, which she'd worn today since she wouldn't be working. She disabused herself of that notion, removing her earplugs and holding the watch to her ear.

The tick was subtle, as might be expected from Cartier.

But the ticking in this chamber was more Bulova, loud and harsh, and not emanating from her wrist.

Somewhere in this chamber, she felt, she *knew*, was a clock – possibly a standard alarm clock – attached to an explosive device. Sticks of dynamite, maybe. Or one of these new plastic explosives.

In a way, she knew – chilled by the thought – that she was herself essentially *within* a sort of bomb, intended almost certainly to explode while the President was on site...assassinating FDR in the most public and humiliating way, taking him out even as the enemy destroyed a defense plant and decimating all its workers.

She yelled for help – which would have been anyone's natural instinct, but Fancy only did so for a short time. She knew these tunnels were empty; she knew no one above could hear her.

"Stop being a baby," she said to herself aloud.

So you're locked in a room, she thought. *What are you going to do about it?*

Taking stock, her hands fell to her tool belt, and she smiled – a tight, Cheshire cat's smile.

That fool Dawson had just knocked her out, shoved her in and shut and locked the doors. That he'd left her with a belt of tools she might make use of he'd obviously overlooked.

With her hammer and a screwdriver, she popped the pins out from the bottom of each hinge, starting with the door at the left; then she did the same with the one at right. Gripping the side-by-side inner knobs, she shimmied the doors up and lifted them off their hinges.

The things were heavy as hell and she had a bad moment when she thought their overwhelming weight might fall on top of her and squash her on her back like a bug. But Fancy had already been a physically fit young woman before spending two weeks riveting and bucking, and she was able to slide the still locked-together, off-their-hinges doors off to one side, and lean them against the wall.

Breathing hard, sweating in a most unfeminine way, she again took stock.

Light from the tunnel, albeit modest, came in and finally she could see the ticking bomb, sitting high atop the stacked drums in back, a six-sticks-black-taped-together affair utilizing, yes, a traditional alarm clock. Nothing fancy, but nothing Fancy could risk trying to defuse.

How much damage can six sticks of dynamite do? she wondered.

Certainly it would create a bigger bomb out of that gasoline, and probably the fire would spread to the other storage chambers and it was not hard to imagine a blossom of orange and black flame emerging from atop Building Four, incinerating the little fake Hollywood town on the roof and eradicating the plant and everyone in it, possibly spreading to a number of the other fourteen buildings on the Amalgamated grounds.

She could see her wristwatch now – just under an hour remained before the President's scheduled arrival.

Good, she thought. *There's time.*

Footsteps echoing like rapid gunfire, she ran down the tunnel to the stairwell door, found it unlocked and went quickly up. She found the plant blissfully unaware of the bomb in its bowels, the many women and the few men at their usual hard, noisy work. Busy ants unaware of the giant picnicker's shoe about to crush them.

Breathing hard, the gas odor still fouling her nostrils, she looked frantically around, within seconds spotting one of the men wearing a dark business suit, so out of place here, positioned near the caged stockroom.

She went to him.

"Sir," she said, "I'm going to assume you're part of the detail assigned to protect the president."

About thirty, he had a blandly handsome face that seemed to have been little used; his frown might have been the first time it ever got wrinkled.

His tone was flat yet crisp, his eyes cold and hard and sharp: "Who told you that today's visitor might be the President?"

"My name is Francine Anders and I'm an investigator working undercover for Douglas Lockhart of Amalgamated. A saboteur just locked me in a storage room filled with gasoline drums and six sticks of TNT rigged to blow. You need to call the nearest bomb disposal unit and evacuate this building. And I would suggest canceling the President's visit."

His expression during her little speech changed from irritated to doubtful to convinced.

"Show me," he said, and took her by the arm, already moving them toward the unlabeled door between the Gents and Ladies.

She led him down the stairs into the tunnel and to the storage room in under two minutes; of course, they were both running.

The federal man stood at the gaping space where the double doors had been. "How did you get out of there?"

"I hammered the pins out of the hinges. Maybe you should skip the questions and clear this building."

He turned to her. "Thank you, Miss Anderson."

"Anders. With Anders Confidential Inquiries. Check that with Lt. Richard Hinder of the LAPD. May I see *your* identification?"

That rocked him back, just a bit, but he grinned. First time for that, too, maybe. "Ronald Parker," he said. "FBI."

He showed her his credentials including his badge.

She said, "All right. I'm leaving this to you."

"Wait at the Administration Building. We're going to want to talk to you."

She nodded and headed out, cutting over to the central aisle so she could walk past Department 190. Joe Dawson might still be in the building – he had time before he needed to leave, and should anyone survive this day, he'd want to have been seen somewhere around the several planes whose construction he supervised.

But there was no sign of him. He could be up inside one of the shells of a ship, pretending to be helpful; but that, unfortunately, was something she couldn't know unless she took time to crawl up inside each one and check. With an announcement to evacuate coming very soon, doing so was not a good use of her time.

The loud speaker began telling everyone to leave the building in an orderly fashion just as Fancy exited. Word was spreading to the men in dark suits and the soldiers in tan khaki, some with walkie talkies, who were moving toward the plant that soon everyone else would be fleeing.

While she paused at the Administration Building, loud speakers repeating the voice-of-God instructions, she did not go in and wait there, as she'd been advised. She had a hunch, a hunch she could act upon if she was quick about it. Because in minutes, no, *moments,* the evacuation would be in full sway and people would be streaming out through Building Four and then every other structure on the grounds, getting the hell away from they-didn't-know-what, just that it must be something serious, really, really serious.

This was wartime, after all.

And anyone with a vehicle would be flooding into the parking lot as everyone but soldiers and federal agents undertook a mass exodus.

Right now, though, just for a very little while, that parking lot stretching before her as she exited the front gates was a mass of cars and no people. Seldom did anyone access their cars during shift – the lot thronged with arrivals and departures, when those times came, but otherwise it was a sea of sleeping automobiles.

That was her hunch – that, with any luck, one person would be in that lot right now, and with just a little more luck she might be able to spot – and catch up – with him.

And there he was.

Dead ahead in the six-thousand-vehicle lot, about a third of the way up the row – the loud speaker warnings not making it all the way out here – Dawson had a head start, with no idea that anyone would be after him yet, calling no attention to himself by running or even walking quickly.

Fancy had no such concern, and she ran, drawing the hammer from her tool belt like a gunfighter's six-shooter, and charging toward the unsuspecting leadman.

But when Dawson paused to edge sideways between two parked cars, to unlock his own, he finally noticed Fancy coming, barreling toward him like a linebacker zeroing in on a quarterback.

Those squinty eyes opened as wide as they could and he got the Baby Browning out of a jumpsuit pocket and was about to train it on her when she was all but on top of him, swinging the hammer, the side of it whapping him alongside the head, about where earlier he had hit her.

He crumpled and she snatched the gun off him.

A security guard had caught wind of it and came up, his revolver drawn.

"Do you have handcuffs?" she asked the guard.

He looked confused, but said, "Yes. But...put that gun down! What's going on?"

She handed the little automatic toward him and he took it with his free hand, still looking puzzled.

"They're evacuating Building Four," she said. "Maybe you know that. This is the saboteur who planted the bomb. Cuff him and keep him in custody."

She stayed long enough to see the security guard snap on the cuffs and haul the groggy Dawson to his feet, then started off, quickly.

"Where are you going?" the guard called, befuddled.

"Where the FBI told me to," she said.

The counselor's office door, as advertised, was open.

Longtin was on her feet, behind her desk, shoving some papers into a briefcase. Her expression mingled alarm and anger as Fancy entered and shut herself in.

"We've been told to evacuate," Longtin said.

"We're far enough from Building Four to be out of harm's way, for now at least. Sit down."

The woman frowned. "Who are you to give me orders?"

"Sit, lady. Or I'll sit you down."

Longtin thought about it. She was almost as tall as Fancy and had a few pounds on her; but also a few years.

She sat. "What in God's name do you think you're doing?"

"Taking you into custody for questioning."

Longtin's laugh was mocking. "On what grounds? Under whose authority?"

"Suspected accessory to murder. Possible conspirator in acts of wartime sabotage – probably treason. As for my authority, I represent the Anders Agency. I'm an operative for a licensed investigator – my father."

"Young lady, we have been instructed, on federal authority, to evacuate this facility. I suggest—"

"I suggest you just listen for a while. I believe Rose Hannold came to you about Joe Dawson trying to recruit her to, shall we say, service servicemen. Rose wasn't the loose girl some thought, and she reported her leadman's illegal behavior to someone she trusted – you. And you told Dawson, and that got Rose killed."

"Rose fell."

"Maybe, and then Dawson finished her off, with his wrench. Or did he push her off that platform and *then* finish her off? Perhaps she really hit her head – after he pushed her. We may never know the details. Happening during the 'lunch' break as it did, no one witnessed it."

Longtin seemed almost amused. "Why would I betray Rose to Dawson?"

"Because he's your accomplice, working to undermine the war effort in ways ranging from prostitution to sabotage. I think you knew about Rose being chosen for that publicity campaign, which means she'd be investigated and questioned – and what Dawson approached her about would be revealed."

Longtin's shrug was too casual. "You may be right about Dawson. I did hear rumors about him, which I was preparing to act upon. But honestly, Miss Anders – why would you think I had anything to do with any of this?"

"Because just this morning I told you about Dawson signing women up for a hooker army. And you knew the President was coming today, probably one of the few here who did...giving you an assassination opportunity that would make your Axis masters very pleased with you and your work."

Longtin's smile verged on a sneer. "You really *don't* have anything, do you? Just guesswork, coincidences, assumptions..."

"Well, I have a few things I can point to. When I told Dawson that I'd informed both you and Lula Hall about his flesh-peddling, he said 'Good to know' about Lula...*not* you. And you obviously contacted Dawson right after I came clean about my identity, and what I knew. Which prompted him to risk grabbing me to get me out of the way."

"It's not enough."

"It's enough to get the feds to look good and hard at you. For now, Miss Longtin, we'll find someone to hold you for questioning."

"You can try," she said, shrugging again, "although I'd imagine everyone is busy at the moment. But I do look forward to suing you for defamation of character."

The counselor gathered her briefcase, came around the desk, and paused at the door.

"After you," Fancy said.

They were barely outside the office when Longtin swung the briefcase into Fancy, who lost her balance, going down on her backside with a *whump*, the tools on her belt clanging on the hardwood floor. Longtin kicked her in the side, where Dawson had hit her earlier; then snatched a small automatic pistol from the fallen briefcase.

Still, Fancy was on her feet in a few seconds, just long enough for the counsellor to make the trip down a short hall and through an EXIT door.

Taking pursuit, Fancy found herself on a landing with both up and down options – and certainly Longtin was heading down.

But then the clacking of high heels came from above in the stairwell. Fancy followed and went through a door to a rooftop where awaited the miniature neighborhood that Hollywood had provided. Camouflage netting was draped over the mini-roof of the enclosed door, extending over the spaces between buildings that also wore fake mini-cities.

White "streets" were painted between rows of faux-homes, which came only knee high, like squat, otherwise oversize dollhouses. But this would provide enough cover for Longtin to crouch out there, somewhere – with her little gun ready.

Why had the woman sought escape up here? Had it been

thoughtless panic? Just sheer survival instinct? But how Fancy's quarry figured to survive taking this route was anybody's guess....

Could there be access to a fire escape whose position was unknown to Fancy, or had this been a maneuver designed to draw her here to be a target? If this rooftop provided no exit, perhaps Fancy should rig some way to lock the door and essentially cage Longtin up here for the feds.

Instead, staying low, wrench in hand, Fancy moved through the little fabricated neighborhood past trees of chicken wire and feathers, shielded by the small plywood structures. Coming to an intersection, she looked both ways, not for traffic – the only "cars" pint-sized ones in driveways and along curbs – but for her prey. So down one street and another, Fancy duck-walked, finding no counselor, stopping at each intersection, and still no Longtin.

Could the woman have crawled across the netting to another rooftop mini-neighborhood, and escaped down the stairs of that *building? Enough of this....*

Fancy stood.

Like a female Gulliver in coveralls, she loomed above the little town, on the hunt for a hiding Lilliputian.

And then there she was.

The dress of her suit hiked over sheer stockings, her once perfect hair an animal tangle, her high heels abandoned in the chase, Longtin crawled like a big spider across the camouflage netting on her way to the adjacent building, gripping as she went, a slow but steady process of escape.

Fancy stepped over houses, brushing by waist-high trees, tiny cars crushed underfoot as she yelled, "Give it up! There's nowhere to go!"

The fugitive rolled onto its back, the attractive face contorted into something no more human than the creature she'd become. The little gun swung toward the pursuer but, before the woman could fire, Fancy flung the wrench and it flew straight and true, its jaw end striking Longtin in the forehead, hard, crunching bone. A blossom of blood dissolved into a scarlet mask housing round white eyes.

The gun dropped from her fingers and she lay there, bouncing on the netting, a spider no longer, just some lesser bug caught in the web.

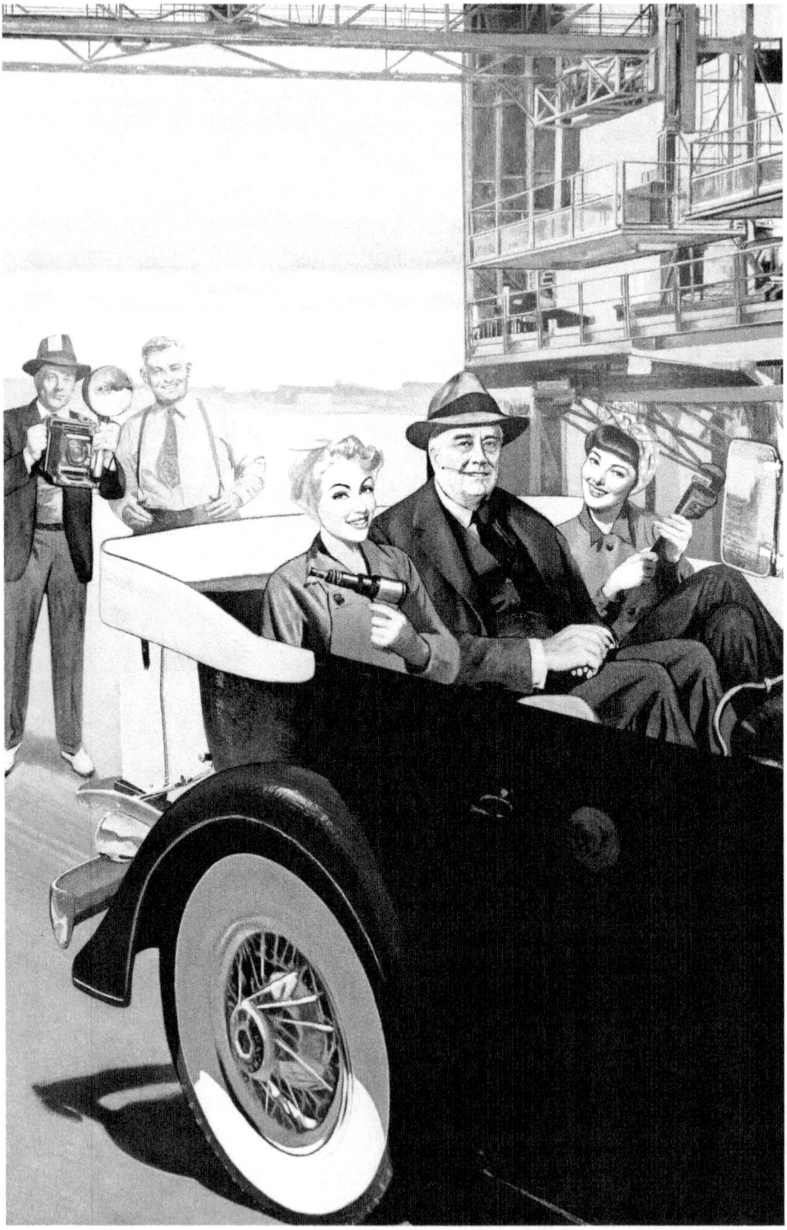

10

END OF SHIFT

The L.A. County Sheriff's bomb squad made quick work of the crude if potentially deadly "improvised explosive device," as FBI agent Parker described it to Fancy.

It happened so fast that the evacuation was shut down and only a handful of workers, who'd fled to bus stops, were not able to return to their stations, most of them having gathered to wait in the lanes of the vast parking lot.

Fancy had collapsed and passed out in the lobby of the Administration Building, where she was found after the "all clear" was sounded. Between the blow to her head and being kicked in the side, which had apparently broken at least one rib, she was escorted by a security guard to the infirmary. There her head wound was dressed, her midsection taped up, and she was administered meperidine.

Alone in the infirmary's small ward, back in her coveralls but resting on a hospital bed, she was awake and alert when agent Parker caught up with her, taking a seat beside her.

"You wouldn't happen to know anything," he said, lips barely moving in his bland, blank face, "about a dead woman we fished out of the camouflage netting near Administration. You were found there, I understand."

"That's Sharon Longtin. Head counselor. Dead?"

"Yes. Your doing?"

"Self-defense."

"With a wrench?"

"It was a do-it-yourself kind of situation. You people may want to revisit your vetting process, because I don't think she was working for the same government."

"Why don't you fill me in," he said.

And she did.

He was almost smiling when she finished. He said, "You're certainly a brave young woman. A little foolish, perhaps, but resourceful and brave."

"At least we headed off FDR's visit."

The agent's eyebrows rose. "You don't know the old man. He's insisting on going ahead with it. We wanted to give this whole facility a top-to-bottom shakedown, before rescheduling, but...well, he apparently wasn't kidding about that 'only thing we have to fear is fear itself' stuff. He won't shirk his duty because of a few 'traitorous cowards.'"

She sat up. "Are you saying the photo shoot is on?"

"That's right," he said, eyes narrowing. "You were supposed to be part of that, weren't you?"

"I still am. Make room."

Parker got out of her way as she swung her legs off the bed.

He said, "Are you sure you're up to this?"

"I'm feeling no pain."

"Few are, on meperidine."

He stopped her with a traffic cop's upraised palm.

"Before you go running off," the fed said, "you need to understand that the events of today, from that explosive device to the saboteur you stopped, are classified, or will be soon. Your role in Joseph Dawson's arrest will likely be made public, but with the details remaining confidential – you are just an undercover investigator who gathered evidence leading to an arrest. Otherwise, what we had here is a bomb scare – that's the beginning and the end of it. All falling under—"

"The Espionage Act. I know."

The rest of her B-24 team, she quickly learned, was waiting in the Building Four cafeteria, as before. And that was where she went.

Chatting over coffee, looking surprisingly fresh after the hubbub, the four women sat around the end of a long, otherwise unoccupied table. Fancy was greeted warmly, with enthusiastic smiles all around, though everyone wanted to know where she'd been.

Lula was staring like she'd just spotted a unicorn. "Did you hit Joe Dawson with a hammer in the parking lot?"

"Sounds like a game of Clue," Fancy said, a little embarrassed, which surprised her, as she didn't embarrass easily.

Maggie Mae said, "That's the word around here, girl. They say you smacked him a good one with your trusty little ball-peen."

"Coppers walked him to the brig in cuffs, all hangdog," Ethel said, her make-up holding or perhaps she'd refreshed it.

"Next time," Carmen advised Fancy, "hit him harder."

"Or get a bigger hammer," Lula said.

Everybody laughed except Fancy, who said, "I'm not allowed to say much more, girls. But I can tell you that that creep's been arrested on suspicion of Rose's murder."

All their eyes grew wide, and stayed that way as Fancy revealed the real reason she'd gone to work at Amalgamated, and who she really was. Lula played along, not letting on she'd already known Fancy's secret. None of them indicated they'd ever heard of Fancy Anders before.

So much for needing a secret identity, she thought. Making like Superman when Lois Lane would do.

"We been suspects all along?" Maggie Mae asked.

"No," Fancy said. "Maybe for two seconds. But we became

friends the first day we met, and I hope we still are. That we always will be."

"No argument, sweetie," Ethel said.

Carmen asked, "Are you gonna be part of this photo thing today, Franny...Fancy?"

"If I do, I'll be using my own name. But I'm not sure how my part in investigating Rose's murder is going to be handled. It's not up to me."

"Is it up to him?" Lula asked. She was looking past Fancy, who turned and saw Rick Hinder moving through the otherwise empty cafeteria, fedora in hand. He was smiling like a shy kid.

"He's got it bad for you, honey," Maggie Mae whispered.

"Maybe he just generally likes girls," Fancy told them. "There's four other beauties at this table, after all. Excuse me."

She got up and met Rick halfway, out of ear shot.

He tossed his hat on a nearby table and took both of her hands in his. "Are you okay?"

"I'm fine. Riding high on painkillers."

He let go of her. "That fed Parker gave me the lowdown."

"About me bagging Dawson?"

"I'm in the know all the way – bound by the Espionage Act myself." He grunted a wry laugh. "They had a hell of a time hauling that Longtin dame down, before they could let all you girls get back to work."

"Too bad she's dead."

A nod, a sigh. "That must be tough for you, Fancy. Now you know what killing somebody feels like."

"Oh, it's not that. I'd just rather the G-men would've had a chance at her. Is it the electric chair or a firing squad for treason, I wonder?"

That made him blink. "Well, we may find out after they run that Dawson character through the mill. Listen, I finally got through to Lockhart in D.C., if that's not a moot point."

"No, the photo shoot is on, and I'm considering doing it. What does he say?"

"Your call entirely, Uncle Doug says. But under *your* name."

"That's the only real option at this point."

He took a step closer. "Would it be okay for me to kiss you right now, Fancy? Your girlfriends would get a kick out of it. Be like the end of a movie."

"A corny one. No. Don't you have somewhere you have to be?"

"I do," he admitted with a lopsided grin. "I'm the liaison 'tween all these local departments and Uncle Sam. So, you like being under covers, Fancy?"

"Under*cover*. Go."

He slapped his hat on and went.

"Golly," Carmen said, as Fancy returned, "he's cute."

Everybody seemed to agree with that, but Fancy kept her opinion to herself. Seated again, she gave them – each one of them – a serious look, then made a little speech.

"Before anybody asks," she said, "I'm not staying on at Amalgamated. You women have a job to do, but so do I – and I can do more good for the war effort as a detective right here on the Los Angeles homefront."

Nobody disagreed, and they all smiled – not big smiles, sad ones admittedly. Smiles, though.

Fancy checked her wristwatch. "Shall we go down and make sure our work area is up to Presidential standards?"

They went out together in a group, but as they entered the plant – where all around them work went on in its noisy, grinding way – Lula fell in next to Fancy.

"You do know I hate this job," Lula said.

"I know."

"Would you be ashamed of me if I quit?"

"You mean, would I throw you out of the house?"

"I can stay on?"

"If you come to work for me you can."

Lula smirked. "Why, you got riveting and bucking needs doing?"

"No, and anyway, you hate that, remember? Let me stake you to a top-notch crash course at a secretarial school I know of. And if you don't flunk out 'cause of a bad attitude, a job as my personal assistant will be waiting."

"I'd kiss you," Lula said, "but I don't want you to get any ideas."

President Roosevelt spent two hours at Amalgamated, touring various buildings and assembly lines, inaugurating a two-week, coast-to-coast defense plant swing. Fifteen minutes of those two hours were spent with Fancy's B-24 team.

FDR rode in the back of his Lincoln limousine, the famous "Sunshine Special" convertible, which traveled down Building Four's central aisle, federal agents in business suits fore and aft and along either side, Agent Parker among them. A sailor jogged in tandem, taking pictures for the government; but plenty of photographers from the press padded along the periphery, too.

The women posed with tools in hand at either side of the President, who beamed in the back seat sporting his famous fedora and jaunty cigarette-in-holder. Fancy – in a borrowed turban and posing with a Buck Rogers rivet gun – was next to him, leaning against the side of the car.

"Haven't we met before, young lady?"

"We have."

"Your father is Major Anders, I believe."

"He is."

"Well, I'm going to make sure you get one of these pictures, and I'll sign it to you personally."

"I'll send a signed picture to you, too."

He laughed; he liked that. "On first glance, dear, I thought you might be this Rosie the Riveter I'm hearing so much about."

"No, sir," Fancy admitted. "Never even met her."

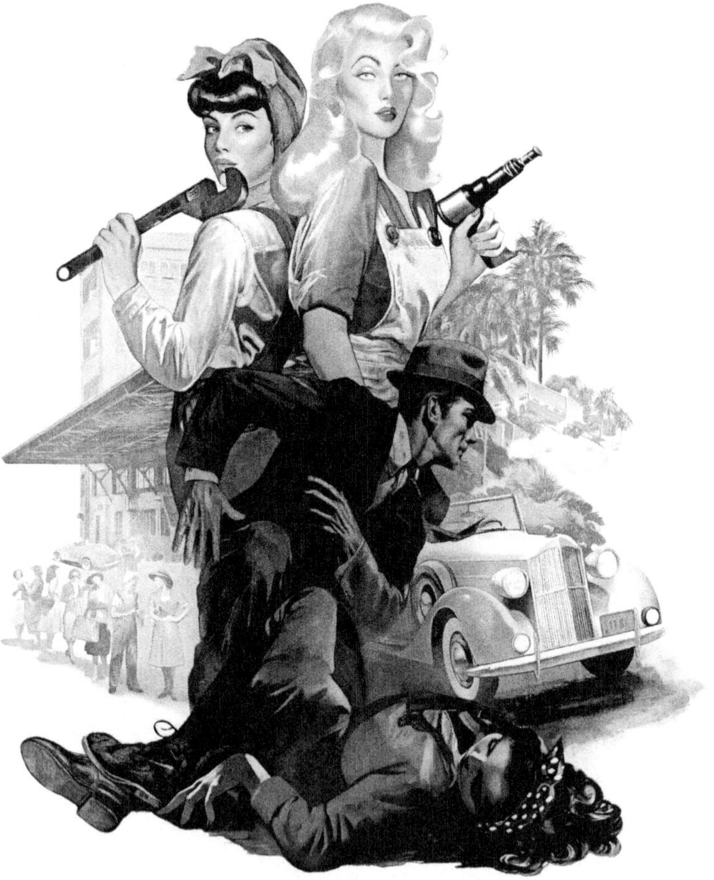

AUTHOR'S NOTE

The aircraft plant in this short novel is a fictional one. Despite efforts to honor history, certain liberties have been taken.

In addition to extensive Internet research, I consulted the following sources: *From Coveralls to Zoot Suits* (2013), Elizabeth R. Escobedo, focusing on the experiences of Hispanic women during World War II; *Rosie the Riveter in Long Beach* (2008), Gerrie Schipske, a photo history and part of the excellent *Images of America* series; *Rosie the Riveter Revisited* (1987), Sherna Berger Gluck, an invaluable oral history; and *Slacks and Calluses* (1944), Constance Bowman Reid (writer) and Clara Marie Allen (illustrator), an entertaining contemporary memoir by two teachers who spent the summer of 1943 working at an aircraft plant in San Diego.

ABOUT THE AUTHOR

MAX ALLAN COLLINS was named a Grand Master in 2017 by the Mystery Writers of America. He is a three-time winner of the Private Eye Writers of America "Shamus" award, receiving the PWA "Eye" for Life Achievement (2006) and their "Hammer" award for making a major contribution to the private eye genre with the Nathan Heller saga (2012).

His graphic novel *Road to Perdition* (1998) became the Academy Award-winning Tom Hanks film, followed by prose sequels and several graphic novels. His other comics credits include the syndicated strip "Dick Tracy"; "Batman"; and (with artist Terry Beatty) his own "Ms. Tree" and "Wild Dog."

His innovative Quarry novels were adapted as a 2016 TV series by Cinemax. His other suspense series include Eliot Ness, Krista Larson, Reeder and Rogers, John Sand, and the "Disaster" novels. He has completed twelve "Mike Hammer" novels begun by the late Mickey Spillane; his audio novel, *Mike Hammer: The Little Death* with Stacy Keach, won a 2011 Audie.

For five years, he was sole licensing writer for TV's *CSI: Crime Scene Investigation (*and its spin-offs*)*, writing best-selling novels, graphic novels, and video games. His tie-in books have appeared on the USA TODAY and *New York Times* bestseller lists, including *Saving Private Ryan, Air Force One,* and *American Gangster*.

Collins has written and directed four features and two documentaries, including the Lifetime movie *Mommy* (1996) and *Mike Hammer's Mickey Spillane* (1998); he scripted *The Expert*, a 1995 HBO World Premiere and *The Last Lullaby* (2009) from his novel *The Last*

Quarry. His Edgar-nominated play *Eliot Ness: An Untouchable Life* (2004) became a PBS special, and he has co-authored two nonfiction books on Ness, *Scarface and the Untouchable* (2018) and *Eliot Ness and the Mad Butcher* (2020).

Collins and his wife, writer Barbara Collins, live in Iowa; as "Barbara Allan," they have collaborated on sixteen novels, including the "Trash 'n' Treasures" mysteries, *Antiques Flee Market* (2008) winning the *Romantic Times* Best Humorous Mystery Novel award of 2009. Their son Nathan has translated numerous novels into English from Japanese, as well as video games and manga.

ABOUT THE ILLUSTRATOR

FAY DALTON is a London-based illustrator best known for The Folio Society's James Bond series and comic covers for Dynamite and Titan's Hard Case Crime. Combining traditional drawing and painting methods with digital painting Fay's work is detailed and boasts a vintage quality, reminiscent of the pulp era. She has also worked on advertisement campaigns for Virgin, Agent Provocateur as well as work for Warner Bros and recently Magic the Gathering.

ABOUT THE PUBLISHER

NeoText is a publisher of quality fiction and long-form journalism. For regular free website articles and information on our latest releases, please visit us at NeoTextCorp.com